Lock Down Publications and Ca$h
Presents

MONEY HUNGRY DEMONS

If you're not at the table you're on the menu.

A Novel By
TRANAY ADAMS

Copyright © 2024 Tranay Adams
Money Hungry Demons

All rights reserved. No part of this book may be reproduced in any form or by electronic or mechanical means, including information storage and retrieval systems without permission in writing from the publisher, except by a reviewer who may quote brief passages in review.

First Edition 2024

Printed in the United States of America

This is a work of fiction. Names, characters, places, and incidents either are products of the author's imagination or are used fictitiously. Any similarity to actual events or locales or persons, living or dead, is entirely coincidental.

Lock Down Publications
P.O. Box 944
Stockbridge, GA 30281
www.lockdownpublications.com

Like our page on Facebook: Lock Down Publications
www.facebook.com/lockdownpublications.ldp

Stay Connected with Us!

Text **LOCKDOWN** to 22828 to stay up-to-date with new releases, sneak peaks, contests and more…

Like our page on Facebook:
Lock Down Publications

Join Lock Down Publications/The New Era Reading Group

Visit our website:
www.lockdownpublications.com

Follow us on Instagram:
Lock Down Publications

Email Us: We want to hear from you!

PROLOGUE

Chick read her son a bedtime story until he'd fallen asleep. She kissed him on the cheek, whispered, "I love you," and returned the novel to its rightful place on the bookshelf. Pulling the door closed behind her, she journeyed down the hallway, where she passed a rectangle shaped mirror, upon entering the living room. She doubled back and took a good look at herself. Her pouty-lips formed a smile as she took in her appearance. Chick was a slender chocolate piece with a mole at the corner of her top lip. She had two handfuls of breasts, a teardrop ass and shoulder length hair, which she kept in box braids.

Chick did a 360-degree turn, loving the reflection of the woman staring back at her. She was about to head into the kitchen to pour herself a glass of white wine, when the doorbell rang. Her brows wrinkled, wondering who it could be at her door at that hour. She stole a glance through the blinds and rolled her eyes, once she saw who it was at the door.

"Fuck does this bitch want?" Chick took an exasperated breath as she walked to the front door. "Shirvetta, you mind telling me why you're at my door at 10:30 at night? And don't gimme any shit about what Golden need, 'cause I swear 'fore God I'm sicka that lame ass excuse." Her eyebrows dipped and she folded her arms across her chest.

"Nah, nothing like that. I just needa talk to you," Shirvetta replied.

"That's what they made phones for. You coulda called. You already know how I feel about folks dropping by unannounced," Chick told her. "As a matter of fact, trick, who do you think you're foolin'? You know Heavy usually makes it home around this hour. You tryna make sure you run into him, huh? You think yo' ass is so slick."

"Girl, please, this ain't got nothing to do with me and our baby daddy. I'm here in hopes to have a discussion that will put this beef between you and me to bed," Shirvetta assured her. "It's in our best interest to put our differences behind us and raise our children together, 'cause like it or not, they're siblings and they will be in each other's lives. Heavy won't have it any way else."

Chick bowed her head and thought about the situation. Everything Shirvetta was saying was straight up. They were going to be in each other's lives, whether they wanted to or not. Heavy was big on family and wouldn't, under any circumstances, allow his children to be raised apart. He'd kill them both, and raise his children himself, before he let that happen.

Chick glanced at the clock on the wall. It was now 10:35. Heavy got off his security gig at 10:30 and he usually made it home around 11 o'clock. She figured she'd give Shirvetta a few minutes to speak her piece, then have her leave before he got home.

"Alright, you've got fifteen minutes, so I suggest you make it count," Chick told Shirvetta, as she undid the last lock and pulled open the door.

"Thank you," Shirvetta said, stepping through the door, clutching her purse and holding her pregnant belly. Her hair was a mess and she had pink glassy-eyes. On top of that, the snot peeking out of her nostrils had dried and crusted.

Shirvetta stood aside as Chick closed and locked the door behind her. When she turned around, Shirvetta was pointing a pistol with a silencer on it at her face. Her top lip peeled back in a sneer and fresh tears burst from her eyes, spilling down her cheeks. Chick fought back the initial shock and mad dogged Shirvetta.

"I should have known yo' slimy ass would pull something like this." Chick's nostrils flared.

"I'm willing to do any and everythang I have to in order to keep my kids and my man."

"Yo, man? Bitch, are you delusional?" Chick looked at her like she was bat shit crazy. "Heavy has been my nigga since junior year of high school. You were my best friend. You're the one that started fuckin' 'em behind my back and winded up gettin' pregnant. Y'all betrayed me, remember?"

Chick took two steps forward but stopped in her tracks when Shirvetta cocked back the hammer of her stick.

"Yeah, I remember. You took 'em back and kicked my ass to the curb. What type of shit is that?"

"Of course, I took my nigga back. We've got a son together, and now we're engaged," Chick replied.

Shirvetta's eyes locked onto the platinum, 8k diamond engagement ring on her finger and her heart shattered like the windshield of a cheating boyfriend's car.

The moment Shirvetta's eyes latched onto her engagement ring, Chick seized the opportunity to take action. She smacked the gun out of her face and it discharged, shattering a nearby lamp. Chick rushed Shirvetta and they wrestled for control of the gun.

"Yo' scandalous ass gon' come to my house and threaten me behind some dick that wasn't yours in the first fuckin' place, how dare you." Chick grunted and clenched her jaws, veins bulging on her forehead.

"Ain't my fault you don't know how to keep a fuckin' man." Shirvetta grunted with a balled up face. She was slowly losing the battle for control of the gun.

The women's shadows danced across the walls as they fought over the pistol. They knocked over furniture and vases, and a portrait fell off the wall before the weapon fired again. Instantly, the racket they were causing stopped. Chick, looking shocked, staggered back holding her stomach. She looked at her hand and it was bloody. A shocked look was on

Shirvetta's face. She looked at the smoking gun in her hands and then at the hole she'd put in Chick's belly. Chick became angry all over again. Her face scrunched and she charged at Shirvetta, screaming. Shirvetta lifted her pistol again, aimed, and fired twice.

Chapter 1

"Yeaaaah, lil nigga, I hope you ready for this ass whippin', 'cause you damn sho' earned it," Curtis cracked the knuckles on his big hairy fists as he brought up the rear, behind the two inmates. Curtis was a five-foot-eleven nigga, with a golden-brown complexion, hazel-green eyes and a reddish-brown goatee. He was a corrections officer at a correctional facility that housed some of the most hardcore criminals the state ever had the misfortune of trying to rehabilitate.

"Yo, Curt, you sho' about this? I've seen the youngin' get busy. I'ma keep it a hunnit and ten witchu, bruh, that mothafucka nice with his hands." Joelle said to his coworker as they made their way down the corridor. He was a caramel complexion dude, with a long head and a receding hairline. He had a dinky mustache and chin hair. Whereas, Curtis was stocky and built like a fucking wrestler, Joelle was tall and slender.

"I don't give a rat's ass. I'ma put this punk inna hurt locker," Curtis assured him, shadow boxing, while walking ahead. His eyes were pinned on the back of the nigga he was about to squabble with. "I told this nigga brother to stay away from my wife, but he wouldn't listen. So now his people gots to pay, and they've gotta pay me in blood, and plenty of it."

Joelle looked at him like, *All right now, I'm trying to tell you.* "I'ma just hope you didn't let cho mouth write a check that cho ass can't cash."

Curtis rolled his eyes as he continued shadow boxing. "Joe, do me a favor, shut the fuck up."

Up ahead, the two felons were walking side by side. One was older and taller while the other was younger and shorter. Both equally as dangerous, their violent modus operandi were proof of this.

"You nervous, son?" Heavy asked his boy. He was a baldhead brother with an almond hue and a graying five o'clock shadow. He stood a whopping six-foot-one. He was big and intimidating. He'd gotten his name on the account of his being 350-pounds, but during his stretch he managed to transform that fat into muscle.

Heavy grew up in Long Beach on 21st and Locust. He gained notoriety as a brawler in his neighborhood from the ridiculous amount of fools he'd knocked out. One of his big homies noticed the potential he had and took it upon himself to help him hone his boxing skills into something beautiful. Heavy had developed a nice knuckle game, but he found the streets far more appealing than being a professional fighter, so he left those aspirations behind.

Heavy had taken Golden under his tutelage when he was just four-years-old, teaching him everything he knew about boxing. Though the boy was a slow learner, once he got the hang of it, he became good enough to knock out grown ass men.

Golden frowned and twisted his lips, giving his old man the side eye. "You can't be serious, pop. I'm 'bouta beat the dog shit out this pig. Word to everythang I love," he swore, rolling his head around on his shoulders then shadow boxing as well.

Heavy gave him a one sided grin. "I'm just fuckin' witchu, baby boy. You know I know what the business is."

"A'ight, this is it, this is where I'ma leave you laid the fuck out, boy." Curtis swore as they entered the laundry area. He removed his utility belt and uniform shirt, and strapped on black gloves. His hairy chest and man-boobs were on full display. He bounced around, fighting an imaginary opponent, while Joelle stood nearby, holding everything he'd just removed.

Golden had stripped down to his undershirt. He was looking over his shoulder at Curtis while Heavy strapped his black gloves over his hands. The gloves were worn so there wouldn't be any bumps and bruises from the fight that would alert the prison staff.

"All right, son, show 'em the consequences of fuckin' with a King," Heavy told him, smacking him on his back.

"If you're done with the theatrics, I'd like to get this shit out the way. I've got things to do," Golden told Curtis, bouncing around, shadowing boxing.

Curtis turned around to Golden, looking like Mike Tyson in his heyday. "I'ma beat the brakes off yo' ass, lil nigga, give that brother of yours somethin' to look at when you get home."

"Come get some, big boy," Golden said, throwing up his gloved fists.

Without warning, Curtis charged Golden, throwing a combination of haymakers trying to take him out of the fight quickly. With his arms at his sides, Golden swiftly avoided the attack he'd launched. Curtis wound up wearing himself out trying to land a solid blow. Not only was his big ass panting heavily with exhaustion, he was sweating like he'd ran a few laps. Golden knew it was all over for him then. Old Curtis was spent, while he, on the other hand, was just getting started. Golden danced around Curtis, sticking and moving, turning his face black and blue. Any time Curtis attempted to throw a punch, he avoided it with expertise and hit him with what looked like four counter punches.

Curtis's eye swelled shut, and he was bleeding from his nose and mouth. He knew he was losing the brawl and it was pissing him off. He got as mad as a bull would, facing a matador. Growling, he charged at Golden full-speed ahead. Golden jumped up and kneed him in the face, fracturing his nose. Curtis stumbled backward hastily. Before he could right himself, Golden was flying across the room and kicking him in the chest. Curtis crashed to the floor and skidded across it, bumping against one of the industrial sized washers. He lay on his back with his eyes in slits, moaning, face looking like raw bloody meat.

"Punk ass nigga," Golden, keeping his eyes on a defeated Curtis, spat off to the side.

"I don't know what story you're gonna make up for dude, but it betta be a damn good one." Heavy told Joelle. "He's gonna have a lotta eyes on 'em with his face all busted up like that."

"I'll think of something," Joelle replied, kneeling down to check the pulse in Curtis' neck. He'd gone still for a moment and he needed to be sure he was still alive.

Heavy nodded, threw his arm around Golden's shoulders and led him out of the laundry room.

***

"I never expected this day to roll around so fast, but here we are." Heavy told Golden from where he was reading on the top bunk. The reading glasses he wore made him look like a university professor.

"Yeah, here we are. Sooooo, any parting words of wisdom for your middle child?" Golden replied, slipping on his wife beater. He was looking at himself in the stainless steel mirror while getting dressed for his departure from prison.

"Work on becoming a better criminal, nigga. I don't wanna have to see yo' black ass back in here again."

Golden grinned as he slipped his LeBron James Cavaliers jersey over his head and fixed it to his liking. "Gee, Dad, thanks."

"Aye, man, on such short notice, that's the best a nigga could do." Heavy said, laying his book down beside him and placing his glasses on top of it. He sat up on his bunk and looked at his son as he got dressed.

"Well, old man, you gave it a shot." Golden told him. He sat on his bunk and started putting on a brand new pair of King James. There was silence as both men were roped in their thoughts. Abruptly, Heavy jumped down from the top bunk when Golden stood upright after tying up his sneakers.

"On a more serious note, son, you're gonna sit at the head of the table of this family. Cowboy is too strung out on that shit to be much of a leader, but then again, the boy's never been one for leadership any damn way," Heavy informed him.

"I thought ma was holdin' shit down, pop." Golden inquired with a frown.

"She is, Golden, but women don't do too well under the pressure of what I'd like to call men's work," Heavy explained. "They aren't built to hold such a position, not for long, anyway. My pop was old school. His pop was old school. Your old man is old school. Love men were made to lead, and their women were made to follow."

Golden nodded understandingly. "I feel you, pop."

"Good. So, when you get out there, you run things how you were taught to and see to it that our family flourishes in whatever we choose to do. You hear me?"

"Don't worry, pop, I'ma hold it down." Heavy grabbed a letter from underneath his pillow and gave it to him. Golden's forehead creased with curiosity, looking at it. It had the pet name his father called his mother written on it, Goddess. "What's this?"

"That's one thang about all my pups, all y'all asses are nosy." Heavy grinned, placing his hand on Golden's shoulder. "Just make sure ya mother gets that, alright?" Golden nodded as he slipped the letter inside his back pocket.

"Love," a corrections officer called for Golden from the doorway.

Heavy looked at the shaved head, Spartan sized white dude and signaled for him to give him a minute. The officer nodded and tapped his digital timepiece, letting Heavy know he was on the clock.

Heavy held Golden's face in his calloused hands as he stared into his eyes. "If you don't know anything else, know that I love you, your sister, brothers and your mother more than anything else in this entire world. Y'all are my life. Never forget that."

A glassy-eyed Golden nodded. Heavy kissed him on his forehead and hugged him. Golden tried to speak but a flood of emotions choked him up so he remained silent. After a moment, he tried to pull away, but his pops held fast, so he hugged him tighter.

"All right, time's up," the corrections officer told Golden.

Golden ignored him and held his father a while longer.

He wanted to give them as much time as they needed in their final moment. "Hey, Love, it's time to go. Do me a favor and move your ass."

"Muthafucka, don't chu see me sayin' goodbye to my fuckin' father?" Golden spat, turning around to the corrections officer. Teardrops fell from his eyes and his nostrils flared. He went to approach the corrections officer but his father stepped in his path.

"It's all right, son, it's all right," Heavy assured him. He gave him a quick hug and kissed him on the side of his head. "Now go ahead and get outta here 'fore these people try to keep you."

"I'ma get chu outta here, pop. I swear to God you'll be reunited with us one day." Golden dapped up his father, once again, before grabbing his clear plastic bag and walking out

of their cell. He sized up the corrections officer before making his way down the tier. "Punk-ass muthafucka."
The corrections officer followed behind him shortly.

Chapter 2

Golden strolled out of state lockup with a see-through plastic bag of his personal belongings. The intense sunlight caused him to scrunch his face but he welcomed the warmth of the sun. He'd been gone for five long years, on a robbery charge, and it felt like he was in a time capsule. It was like the entire world was moving along, while he was sitting still. He kept up with everything and everyone through the iPhone he'd secured on lock. It was the best $2,500 he'd spent. Some may have thought he was crazy for spending that much bread on a phone, but the price for everything in prison was significantly higher than it was out on the streets.

Golden smiled for the first time in a long time, since he'd gone away. It felt good as hell to be free and he couldn't wait to get into everything he'd dreamed of while incarcerated. An all-black Mercedes-Benz Sprinter van drove up in front of Golden's eyes. Its windows were pitch-black, so he couldn't see inside of it, but something told him that all the dirt he'd done in the streets had come back to haunt him. His heart thudded mercilessly, and his stomach did somersaults. He was about to reach for his waistband, but then he remembered he was just released from prison and wasn't strapped. Damn.

The doors of the sprinter van popped open. Golden was about to flee for safety, until he recognized the forty-six-year-old woman who appeared before him. He smiled as the five-foot-eight mahogany goddess presented herself. She weighed 155-pounds. Ten of that was tits, and another twenty of it was ass. While her family called her Shirvetta, the streets called her Legs, but Golden and his siblings referred to her lovingly as ma or momma.

"Ma." Golden's eyes lit up and he ran over to his mother. Still holding his clear plastic bag, he scooped her up from the pavement and spun her around like she was a child. She laughed and giggled.

"Boy, put me down 'fore you mess around and drop me." Shirvetta told him. Golden sat her down and she hugged him for what seemed like an eternity. She kissed him all over his face and told him how much she missed and loved him.

"I miss and love you, too, ma. You're my number one lady." Golden replied.

"Boy, look at chu, you done made a thug cry." Shirvetta smiled as tears slid down her cheeks. She took the time to wipe the wetness from her eyes.

Golden stared at his mother and noticed the difference five years made. His mother had always been one stunningly attractive woman, but since she'd taken charge of their family business, she was showing signs of hard living. The stress of running the streets and trying to keep things in order had gotten the best of her. The slight wrinkles on her face and the crow's feet at the corners of her eyes represented this well. The faint traces of scars on her forehead and chin did, too. Then, there were her eyes. A person's eyes always told what someone was trying to hide. Still, she wouldn't dare complain about the amount of pressure she was under. Madukes had entirely too much pride to admit something like that.

"Look at me hoggin' up my baby. Where are my manners? I know your brother and sister wanna welcome you home. Come on." Shirvetta told Golden, ushering him over to his younger brother and sister, who were posted up beside the grill of the Mercedes Sprinter van.

"My young bull, done got big on me," Golden smiled as he slapped hands with his baby brother, Biggie. He shook up with him and gave him a brotherly hug.

Biggie was nineteen-years-old and stood five-foot-seven. He was brown-skinned with abstract designs cut into his fade. He'd gotten his nickname on the account he was a whopping twelve pounds and eight ounces when he was born. Biggie was a chubby little dude but he didn't have a complex about his weight. He didn't see it as a problem because his size never stopped him from getting two of his favorite things in life, money and pussy.

"Welcome home, big bruh." Biggie smirked, hugging Golden.

Frowning, Golden broke their embrace and lifted up Biggie's shirt. He had two guns in his waistband. "Damn, bruh, it's like that?"

"You know how we're livin' out here, bro. Besides, I rolled out with the queen and the princess today. I gotta be dangerous if I'ma hold them down, nah mean?" Biggie said, adjusting his guns in his waistband.

Golden nodded and hugged his brother again. He was overprotective of the women in his family, just like he and their father.

Golden looked over his brother's shoulder and saw his little sister, Baby Girl. She was smiling and tears were twinkling in her eyes. Before he knew it, she ran over and jumped into his arms. She held him tightly as tears burst out of her eyes and slicked her cheeks. He rubbed her back comfortingly as she sobbed into his chest. Baby Girl didn't have to say anything. He knew she missed the hell out of him.

Golden kissed Baby Girl on top of her head. His forehead wrinkled when he looked around and didn't see his oldest brother, Cowboy. He looked over his shoulder at Shirvetta and Biggie. Sorrowful looks spread across their faces, and they lowered their heads. They didn't know how to go about breaking the news to him.

"Ahem," Shirvetta cleared her throat with her fist to her mouth. "Baby, your brother couldn't make it. You see, Cowboy—"

Golden threw up his hand, cutting off what his mother had to say. "Momma, I want you to save your breath for whatever lie you're about to spin on Cowboy's behalf. From what I hear, ya oldest has been so busy pumpin' that poison into his veins, he hasn't found the time to squeeze in to see his lil bruh."

"Golden, your brother is an addict," Shirvetta began to explain. "You know as well as anyone that once people get hooked on drugs, they're not the—"

"With all due respect, ma, I'm not tryna hear any more dialogue in your attempt to defend Cowboy's choices." Golden said. "I'll holla at 'em whenever I run into 'em. I'm a free man. It's a beautiful day. I've got you and the twins here," he took his siblings under each of his arms. He smirked and they smiled. "I'm not tryna ruin my day with talks of big bruh's support, or lack thereof. Ya heard?" He kissed Baby Girl on the side of her head and hugged Biggie into him.

Shirvetta smiled happily, seeing her children reunited after five years. They all embraced in one big, family group hug.

"I love y'all, word is bond." Golden swore.

"We love you, too, bro." Baby Girl spoke for them all.

"Shit, I almost forgot," Golden said, reaching inside of his pocket. His family exchanged glances and then looked at him curiously. He pulled out a letter and handed it to his mother. Her brows wrinkled, wondering what he was giving her. Seeing the questioning look in her eyes he decided to answer her. "Pop told me to give that to you. He said it was for your eyes only. He said for you to read it once you were alone."

Shirvetta nodded and placed the letter inside of her designer purse.

The honking of a horn made everyone turn around. A royal blue Bentley Continental GT pulled into their line of vision. The sunlight made the vehicle's paint job and custom rims gleam. Golden figured whoever was rolling it was some big time dope boy or an entertainer. The driver honked the horn twice more. Golden frowned, wondering if the driver was there for him. His eyebrows raised and he pointed a finger to his chest. The passenger window rolled down and he was greeted by a smiling face. She tilted her designer shades down and waved at everyone.

"Hey, Biggie. Hey, Baby Girl. Hey, ma," Aries smiled jovially.

"Hey, girl." Baby Girl waved back.

"What up, sis?" Biggie replied.

"Aye, daughter-in-law." Shirvetta smiled and waved back at her.

"Yo, you're still coming out to eat with the fam, right?" Biggie inquired.

"Yep." Aries replied, then looked at Golden. "You rolling with me or yo' fam, daddy?"

"Shiiiit, I'm rollin' witcho fine, rich ass." Golden said, like she should know that.

Aries motioned him over. "Well, come on, Big Daddy, 'less you've got a boyfriend in there you're waiting on." Aries pushed the designer shades back up on her face and pressed a button within the car. The convertible top of the GT balled up like a fist and tucked itself away.

"You got alla jokes today, huh?" Golden asked with a grin.

Golden hugged his family again before jogging towards the $220,000 whip. Aries took him in as he approached her, licking her lips thirstily. At twenty-three-years-old, Golden was five-foot-eleven and weighed a total of 175 pounds. He had an athletic body and nearly every inch of it was covered in tattoos. Although he'd entered through the gates of prison with a mop of dreadlocks, he'd left rocking a kinky Mohawk.

Golden jumped in the passenger seat and tongued Aries down. She pulled back, smiling, and squeezed his third leg in his jeans.

"Mmmm, well, someone's happy to see me," Aries said, licking her top lip seductively.

"Oh, my nigga is more than happy." Golden smiled back.

"I just bet." Aries kissed him again.

The Mercedes-Benz Sprinter van pulled up alongside Aries's whip. The passenger window came down, revealing a jovial Baby Girl.

"Ewww, y'all can save that mess for later, we're tryna get something to eat," Baby Girl told them. Golden and Aries smiled and shook their heads.

"You ain't never lied. I'm hungry as a hostage." Biggie chimed in, rubbing his stomach.

"I see nothin' has changed. Nigga, you always hungry." Golden grinned. "Where we at with it, sis?"

"Your favorite spot, Chubby's, y'all follow us," Baby Girl replied, letting her window up. The Sprinter van drove away and Aries followed behind it. Beyoncé's "Drunk in Love" was pumping from out of its speakers.

***

The family was shocked at how Golden was putting the grub away, when they finally received their meals. The boy was eating like he'd been raised in the wild, among a bunch of fucking savages. The only sounds coming from his area of the dining room table were his munching and his fork hitting the plate. He'd ordered candy yams, mac & cheese, mustard greens, cornbread and smothered pork chops. To wash it all down, he had a cup of what the restaurant called Obama punch, which was really just grape and fruit punch Kool-Aid mixed. It was good as hell though. For dessert,

Golden wanted some banana pudding, but they were all out, so he settled for peach cobbler; one of his favorite desserts.

The rest of the time at the restaurant was spent with the family, catching Golden up with everything that happened since he'd been locked away. He shared him and his father's prison war stories with them, and even some of the comical times they shared. There were jokes and laughter, but then things took a serious turn when Shirvetta chose to take control of the conversation. It creeped out Golden how his mother could be horsing around one minute, and then turn as serious as cancer within the next. It was like she had split personalities.

"Look here, son, I know you just came home, but we could use you on this lil lick we've got planned," Shirvetta began, but stopped short when the waitress returned to the table to see if any of them wanted anything else. Shirvetta declined on everyone's behalf.

"Ma, I'm always hungry and I'm always lookin' to eat. So what's on the menu?" Golden asked with a seriousness in his eyes.

"Chris Stacks," Aries interjected. As soon as she spoke, Golden's head snapped in her direction.

"I heard of homie while I was on lock. What's he workin' with?" Golden asked.

"We're lookin' at two hunnit kay or better. Least that's what our inside woman told us," Shirvetta said, before taking a drink of her beverage.

"Inside woman? Who dat?" Golden frowned.

Shirvetta nodded to Aries, who looked at Golden with a smile, waving at him.

"You still wheelin' em in, huh, mama?" Golden spoke of how he had Aries setting up ballers for him to rob when he was home. He didn't know she had hooked up with his fam bam and was working with them to get at jux.

"Like I was sayin' son, we could use you, if you're up to it. If not, then we'll just try to figure somethin' else out." Shirvetta told him.

"Ma, we're family, so I'm always down, no questions asked." Golden assured her.

"That's my baby." Shirvetta smiled. She walked around the table, kissing him on his cheek and hugging him. Baby Girl and Biggie looked on with smirks, happy to have their brother back working beside them in the family business. All of Shirvetta's kids knew that she loved them all but she had a special place in her heart for Golden, and they were okay with that.

Chapter 3

Cowboy sat on a blue milk crate outside of a bodega, nodding in and out of a heroin induced high. Cowboy was a six-foot-tall, twenty-seven-year-old man. He had light-brown eyes and an almond hue. He'd earned his nickname on the account of the wild stunts he'd pulled growing up. Cowboy was known to do whatever, whenever, for cold cash, but most times it was for the adrenaline rush. The boy was a thrill seeker. While the homies made their coins flipping narcotics, Cowboy made his hitting licks with a crew of misfits not much older than him. He reasoned that while the money from selling drugs was good, sticking up hustlers was a much faster way to earn a dollar.

For as strong and malevolent as Cowboy was, he wasn't a match for heroin. He started off snorting, and then he graduated to the needle. It wasn't long before he started neglecting his responsibilities and wound up homeless, living here and there. He didn't care what he looked like, smelled like, or how he dressed. His sole purpose was to get high and stay high, and that became his reason for jacking mothafuckas.

"Yo, Cowboy. Cowboy," Golden called out to his big brother, with his hands cupped around his mouth. He didn't get a response, so he looked up and down the block for any oncoming cars. When he didn't see any vehicles coming, he jogged across the street and up onto the curb where Cowboy was still nodding. Every now and again, he'd throw his head back, smacking his lips and scratching underneath his chin.

"Nigga, I know you heard me calling yo' bitch-ass." He threw playful punches at him, but he didn't budge. He frowned when he took in his appearance. He'd heard stories about him fucking with heroin while he was locked up, but he didn't know he'd become a full-blown junkie.

"Son, wake yo' punk ass up." Golden smacked Cowboy upside his head, knocking his cowboy hat to the sidewalk. Cowboy jumped to his leather, snakeskin boots in a boxer's stance, throwing up his fists. Golden laughed, seeing his oldest sibling snapping back to the spry young man, who was quick to jump bad. They danced around each other, bobbing, weaving and throwing phantom punches. Abruptly, they busted up laughing, giving each other a thug hug and patting each other's back.

"Bitch, when you fly the coop? And why the fuck didn't chu tell me?" Cowboy laughed, shaking up with Golden and hugging him again.

Golden's face suddenly turned serious, and so did Cowboy's. He dropped his head and scratched the back of his neck. Something he always did when he was lost for the right words. Golden had heard from his big brother a total of three times during his five year stretch. He'd written to him more times than he could count. However, Cowboy was sure to make at least a one hundred dollar deposit every month so he could get the necessities he wanted while incarcerated. Sure Aries was holding him, down but that was what she was supposed to do as his girl. Cowboy was his family, so it was only right he did his part in making sure he was good.

"Look, uh, G, I know you're probably hot at me for not comin' to see you and shit. But chu gotta understand, bro, I got caught up in these streets and—"

Cowboy was cut short by Golden grabbing him by his face and staring into his eyes. Golden wore a scowl and his upper lip was pulled back in a sneer.

"Wrong, muthafucka, you got caught up with that fuckin' needle," Golden spat, exposing the track marks on the inside of Cowboy's arm and smacking them.

Cowboy snatched his arm back and shoved him. He rolled down his sleeve and looked back up at him. His eyes were glassy, and he felt ashamed, knowing he'd let his addiction come between him and his brother.

"Fuck happened to you, son? Huh? The Cowboy I knew woulda never left his brother to rot, but this nigga standing before me did." Golden wore a look of disgust on his face as he looked him up and down. "If it wasn't for the fact that I love you, I'd kick yo' ass up and down this block. But then again, I'd feel bad about putting paws on a no good fuckin' junkie."

As soon as those words left his mouth, Cowboy upped his trusty nickel-plated revolvers. The sunlight reflected off the weapons' barrels as they lingered in their intended victim's face.

Golden had nerves of steel as he looked beyond the pistols and into his brother's eyes. They mad dogged each other.

"Shut up. You shut yo' goddamn mouth," Cowboy spat heatedly.

Golden glanced at Aries, who was hopping out of the Bentley with an Uzi. She surveyed the block waiting for traffic to clear up so she could aid her man. Golden looked back at Cowboy. "You know the rules of the game, big bruh. Once the guns come out, they don't go back in until we've used 'em."

"Trust me, I know. I've gotta good memory." Cowboy assured him, cocking back the hammers of his six-shooters and placing his fingers on their triggers.

"Cowboy, stop. What the fuck are you doing? Y'all are brothers," Aries called out as she ran towards her boo and his brother. She ran up on the curb, lifting her Uzi to lay Cowboy down, if need be. "Cowboy, don't make me do this, bro. You know I got mad love for you, but when it comes to Golden, I'd risk facing the wrath of God."

The tension between Cowboy and Golden was as thick as those big booty strippers at King of Diamonds. They held each other's gaze, wondering what was going to happen next. Then, suddenly, Cowboy put the hammers of his revolvers back in place and tucked them inside of his waistband.

"I've got love for you, lil' nigga," Cowboy told him, snatching up his hat from the sidewalk. "But I swear on everythang that is holy, if you ever call me a junkie, dope-fiend or anythang else, outside of my good Christian name again, I'ma see to it niggas in the hood are smokin' on Golden packs. Ya dig?"

Golden didn't respond but Cowboy knew he'd heard him loud and clear. With that, the oldest of the Love brothers adjusted his hat on his head and walked down the block in the opposite direction. He scratched his arm through his shirt's sleeve.

Aries lowered her Uzi to her side and hugged Golden. He wrapped his arms around her as he stared at Cowboy's back. His face was still solemn but his eyes portrayed the pain deep within his heart. He felt a hot stinging in his eyes, and then tears flooded his cheeks. Aries looked up at him, wearing a frown. Using one of her manicured hands, she wiped the wetness from her man's eyes.

"Everything is gonna be aw'right, boo. I promise. I got us." Aries swore, kissing Golden on his cheek. Taking his hand, she started for the curb, where cars were racing up and down the street. "Come on. I'm sure someone has seen us with these guns out here and called Jake by now."

Damn, son, I never thought I'd see the day me and bruh would come at each other like this. This is some sad ass shit. I could only imagine what moms and pops would say if they saw us just now.

***

The run in with Golden, earlier, had fucked with Cowboy's mental, a lot. He'd been called everything but a child of god by some of everybody he could think of. None of the insults bothered him because they came from people he didn't give a flying fuck about. He also straightened them out with a beating or busting a cap in their ass. Things were different when it came to Golden, though. They used to be the tightest out of all of his mother and father's children. They knew each other's deepest, darkest secrets, as well as likes and dislikes, so his calling him a "junkie" hurt him like a punch to the gut. Had he been anyone else, he would have blown his head off. But his love for him outweighed the animosity he had.

Cowboy felt the lowest of low and the last thing he wanted to be right then was sober, so he scouted out a couple of young niggas doing their thang out of a bando. The work they had wasn't all that, but he was sure it was potent enough to make his worries of today a thing of the past.

Spiiiinnnn, click. Spiiiiinnnnn, click. Spiiiiiinnnnn, click.

The sound of a revolver's cylinder spinning and clicking, over and over again, spooked the dope boys. They jumped up from their posts to hide the dope they had left and retrieve their guns. They knew that whenever they heard those twin six-shooters spinning around, Cowboy had come around looking to take whatever they had worth taking.

Spiiiiinnnnnn, click. Spiiiiinnnn, click. Spiiiiinnnnn, click.

"Y'all niggas hurry up, son. Hurry," one of the dope boys called out to the other, after stashing the last of the work inside of a hidden compartment and pushing the dryer back against it. He pulled his gun out of the small of his back, cocked it and darted back towards the living room, where the other workers had gathered. They were all either cocking their guns or making sure those shits were loaded.

The dope boy, in a hushed tone, gave orders for them to post up at all entrances of the trap. He knew that every way out of the house was a way in, so he needed a man to hold every access point down. The dope boys moved to take up their post. The spinning and clicking of the revolver's cylinder suddenly stopped. And they all froze where they were, looking around frantically.

"Yo, that spinnin' and clickin' shit st—" One of the dope boys was cut short by another shushing him. His brows were creased as he looked around, waiting to hear the spinning and clicking of the revolvers again, but they never came. Instead, he got this—*Ba-boom.*

Splinters flew everywhere as the raggedy ass front door was kicked open. Cowboy stepped through the door, wearing a hat and a black bandana over the lower half of his face. He swung his trusty pistols around the living room, lying mothafuckas down before they could take a shot at him. One by one, the dope boys hollered out in agony as bullets zipped through either their legs or thighs, dropping them wherever they stood. The smell of gunpowder and blood lingered in the air, like the stench from a fart.

Cowboy went around the living room, kicking the guns out of the dope boys reach. Out of the corner of his eye, he saw one of them reaching for his piece, which was inches away. He swung his revolver in his direction and pulled its trigger. The chamber spun, a piping hot slug zipped across the room, blowing two of the dope boys fingers off.

"Aaaaaahhhh." The dope boy threw his head back, hollering and cradling what was left of his mutilated hand. Tears burst out of his eyes and ran down his cheeks.

"Youz a hardhead muthafucka, B. Now you've gotta learn how to jack off with ya left hand." Cowboy shook his head. Using one of his pistols, he knocked the Yankees fitted cap off the dope boy's head and held him at gunpoint. "Where the dope at, nigga? I know y'all done put the shit in another hiding place," he said, thinking about all the times he'd robbed this very trap spot. He'd hit them so many times that he knew all of their names, and they knew his. They were easy pickings for a jack boy of his expertise, so whenever he found himself without any money to cop dope, he'd go and stick their asses up. The dope boy didn't respond, he mad dogged him.

Chapter 4

"Cordare, I'm not gonna ask you again." Cowboy cocked the hammer of his revolver back with his thumb and pressed it right between his eyes. Unbeknownst to him, a thirteen-year-old, brown-skinned kid, wearing a black do-rag and hoodie, crept out of the bedroom behind him, gripping a Tec-9. The other dope boys spotted him but they didn't say a word. They knew he was inside of the bedroom all along. He'd gone inside to take a dump, while they were busy serving fiends.

The little nigga had taken three steps before Cowboy's nose scrunched up from the terrible stench coming from behind him. Without turning around, he stuck his revolver around the opposite side of his trench coat and popped the youngin'. A bullet zipped through the kid's stomach sending him sailing backwards and firing the Tec-9 up at the ceiling. Debris trickled from the ceiling as he slammed up against the wall and dropped his gun. His face balled up in excruciation. His eyes welled up with tears as he held his stomach, blood seeping between his fingers.

"Nearly caught me slippin', lil nigga. Luckily for me, I caught a whiff of yo' funky ass before I saw you." Cowboy told the teenage dope boy he'd slumped against the wall. "Cordare, you got this kid workin' the trap witchu and he doesn't look old enough to be off his mother's tit." He focused his attention back on the kid he'd dropped. "Youngin', where the trap at? Start talkin' or I'll blow yo' lil wee-wee off before you learn how to use it." He held Cordare at gunpoint, while aiming his other pistol at the teenager's crotch.

The kid looked around at all of the dope boys who were shaking their heads and mouthing to him not to say anything. As bad as he wanted to prove his gangster to the others, the threat of having his delicates blown off before he'd gotten the chance to feel the insides of a woman outweighed his peers' opinion of him. The young dope boy threw his head towards the back of the house.

"It's stashed behind the dryer, inside a—inside a hole in the—in the wall," the teenage dope boy stated, pointing towards the backroom with a bloody hand. His gunshot wound was wreaking havoc on him. He'd already begun to turn pale and sweat like a whore in church.

Cowboy took a look around at all of the dope boys inside of the living room. He only had about three bullets between his two revolvers, should shit go left in there. On top of that, he wasn't anyone's fool. He figured it was in his best interest to send the youngster to recover the drugs they had on deck.

"Gon' head and get it," Cowboy motioned with one of his revolvers. "Lemme warn you though, youngsta, if you come back here with anythang, other than what I sent chu for, I'ma put a bullet in the back of each one of these fuckaz heads. Ya dig?"

Wincing, the teenage dope boy nodded and walked towards the backroom, holding his stomach, dripping blood. A minute later, he returned with a plastic grocery bag loaded with packets of heroin. Cowboy looked at the contents and smiled behind the bandana. He pocketed the stash, spun the pistols around in his hands and bid his victims a farewell. With that, he vanished, on some Batman shit.

Spiiiiiinnnnn, click. Spiiiiinnnnn, click. Spiiiiinnnn, click. Spiiiiiinnnnn, click! Spiiiiiinnnn, click! Spiiiiinnnn, click!

The sound of Cowboy's pistols' cylinders spinning and clicking grew lower and lower, until they were no longer heard. When he was finally out of sight, Cordare pulled out his burnout cellular phone and dialed 9-1-1.

Cowboy found solace inside a trashy basement with cobwebs in every corner and the occasional mouse running around. The place was loaded with cardboard boxes and other miscellaneous items. Still, he didn't complain. It was a roof over his head. The old Puerto Rican lady he was renting the place from provided him with something hot to eat every day. And on top of that, his stay was only running him one hundred and fifty bucks a month. Considering how high the rent was in New York City, he couldn't beat that price with a stick.

Cowboy sat shirtless in a big brown La-Z-Boy reclining chair, fixing himself a shot of dope. Every now and again, he'd glance up at *Good Times,* which was playing on the box television set. The old thing was terribly scarred, with duct tape holding it together and a wire hanger for an antenna, but it worked as good as new.

"Hahahahahahaha. J.J. a muthafuckin' fool, son." Cowboy laughed as he slipped his thick leather belt around his arm, buckled it and pulled it tight with the teeth he had left.

After he'd found a vein, he used a soiled cotton ball to rub alcohol on it and picked up the syringe, squirting some of its contents out of its needle. He was about to inject the heroin into his system until one of J.J.'s antics made him laugh hardily again. Feeling his arm twitch with the indication his demon was ready to be fed, Cowboy stopped fucking around and administered the medication he'd stolen from the street pharmacists. Once he'd pressed the feeder all the way down, he slumped in his chair, with his eyes fluttering, pulling the syringe out of his arm. He allowed it to drop to the floor as he ran his hands up and down his body. He licked his top row of teeth, bit down on his bottom lip and groped the bulge in his gray sweatpants. The sensation he was experiencing was one only an author of an erotic fantasy novel could make up.

***

That night...

Aries drove out to College Point, which was a very peaceful, middle-class, suburban neighborhood in the New York City borough of Queens. She drove up into the driveway of a two-story, four bedroom house, with beautiful flower bushes and a rich, green, manicured lawn. Aries, wearing a big smile, turned off her whip and hopped out. Golden hopped out behind her, slamming the door shut and making his way around the front of the vehicle.

"Sooooo, what do you think?" Aries asked him excitedly. She purchased the house for Golden while he was locked up, but she never told him about it. She figured she'd surprise him instead.

Golden tucked his plastic bag of belongings under his arm as he stared up at the house. "This is nice, real nice. How much you renting this muthafucka for?"

"Rent? Baby, this is ours. I bought this. Come on. Let's take a look." Aries shook the keys at him and grabbed his hand. She led him up onto the porch, where she unlocked the front door. As soon as they walked inside, she flipped on the light switch and locked the door behind them.

"Soooo, what do you think?" Aries asked with a smirk. She walked up beside him, while he looked at the place.

"I can't front, shorty, you did the damn thang. This muthafucka all that and then some." Golden looked at her grinning. She fell into his arms and kissed him slowly and passionately. He ran his hands up and down her back, while they made out.

Scooping her up in his arms, he carried her inside of the master bedroom, where he laid her on the bed and crawled on top of her. She pulled him down on her and they kissed heavily, breathing hard. Their hands got busy undressing each other. Her nipples were rock hard and he'd already bricked up. Before either of them knew it, they were naked and Golden was sliding deep inside of her. Aries's eyes widened and her mouth opened with a gasp. It had been quite some time since she felt him inside of her. Not only did it hurt, but it felt good.

Golden slipped his tongue inside of her mouth, kissing her slowly and deeply. His buttocks moved in a circular motion as he gave her slow, deep strokes, hitting the very bottom of her kitty. She moaned in ecstasy, and turned her head. He licked the thick vein alongside her neck and gently bit on it. He sucked on it. Her eyes fluttered. She moaned louder, encouraging him to go deeper inside of her.

"Deeper, Golden. I want you to go deeper," Aries whispered into his ear, making it hot and moist. She licked his earlobe, and sucked on it like a pacifier.

He obeyed her command, slipping his toned, vein riddled arms under her legs and tooting his butt up. He pulled his pipe out to the tip, then drove it down into her, to his sack. She began whimpering and calling his name, over and over again. It turned him on so much he started fucking her savagely. He went faster and harder inside of her, with each thrust. His nut sack smacked against her sweaty asshole, while his rock hard abs brushed against her clit. This provided more stimulation. Her face balled up. Her eyes turned white. She wrapped her arms around his neck and pulled him closer to her. She bit into his neck and moaned into his ear.

Golden started pumping into her recklessly. The friction he was causing between them made both of them rasp. He would get loud and she, in turn, would get louder. Golden's buttocks flexed with every pump, while her legs bounced up and down.

"Shit. I'm abouta cum, ma. Damn, yo' pussy so, umm, I don't wanna pull out this muthafucka. Grrrr." Golden grunted like a werewolf, sinking his teeth into her neck. She whined like she'd been pierced by a hot spear.

"Cum—cum—cum deep inside of me, baby. I wanna feel—I wanna feel yo' hot seeds deep inside of me. Oh, God, I wanna have yo' baby." Aries cried, tears sliding out the corners of her eyes.

"I want chu to have my baby, too, boo. I'ma make you a mother and my wife. You hear me, ma. All you gotta do is tell me you want it." Golden kissed her and then looked into her eyes. In that moment, she was so fucking beautiful to him; inside and out. He knew then she was the only woman he'd ever want to be with. He didn't need anyone else.

"I want—uh—I want—I want it." Aries replied. The tears didn't seem like they'd ever stop.

Golden kissed her again. They held each other's gaze as he continued to beat up her pussy. They breathed hard into each other's faces. Their bodies shone from sweat sliding down every inch of their forms. Golden closed his eyes and his nostrils expanded. Throwing his head back, he roared like a grizzly and exploded deep inside of her. Grunting, he pumped and pumped, making sure he emptied all he had inside of her. Aries came right after, hollering and shaking uncontrollably.

Golden fell on top of her, exhausted and breathing hard. She kissed him all over the side of his face, and ran her nails up and down his back. When she saw her name inked on the side of his neck, she kissed it and smiled. It made her recall the one she'd gotten of his name behind her right ear in Japanese letters.

"You good, ma?" Golden asked, kissing her under her chin and nibbling on the soft flesh.

"Unh huh," Aries replied, with her eyes closed and a smile.

"You meant alla that stuff you said while we were gettin' busy? Or were you just in the moment?" Golden asked.

Aries eyes popped open and latched onto his. "I meant every last word of it. What about you? Did you mean it?" she asked, tracing his lips with her finger.

"Shorty, I don't say shit I don't mean."

Aries chuckled and smirked. "I love you."

"More than you love that nigga, Rich Loc?"

"I don't love anyone on this planet more than I love you."

"Yeah. Whatever." Golden laid his head against her chest again.

"Babe, I'm serious, look at me," Aries told him. Golden looked up at her. "I'd kill myself before I'd ever hurt you. I love you entirely too much."

"I hope so. I really, really hope so." Golden told her with serious, glassy-eyes.

"Kiss?"

Golden kissed Aries and rolled over on his back. He looked for something to watch on Netflix as she snuggled up beside him and focused her attention on the television. Golden slipped his arm around her shoulders and continued to browse the movie catalog. Being in the streets, Golden accepted the fact he'd wind up dead, catching a body, or a case. It didn't matter which one, because he could handle them all. But what he couldn't handle was getting his heart broken. As strange as it may seem, "love" was the only thing he was deathly afraid of.

Chapter 5

Shirvetta, who wore her hair pinned up, entered the bathroom, wearing a red satin robe with colorful flowers on it. She placed Lavender scented candles around the Jacuzzi-sized tub and lit them one by one. She set her cellphone and the letter Golden had given her on the floor beside the tub. Once she turned off the lights, she slipped out of her robe and let it drop in a pile at her feet. Although Shirvetta was the mother of three, you couldn't tell by looking at her. Shorty didn't look a day over thirty. She had mad sex appeal, and a body that made a nigga want to bust out singing a 90's R&B ballad.

Shirvetta eased into the hot, foamy water, picked her letter back up, and laid back in the tub. The steam of the water already had her face and chest shiny. Taking the manicured pinky of her right hand, she slit open the envelope and pulled out the letter Heavy had written. Butterflies fluttered inside of her stomach, wondering what it was her husband had to say to her. Smirking, she sat the envelope aside on the floor and began reading the words of her incarcerated lover.

What's up, Goddess?

I hope this letter finds you and our litter in the best of health mentally, physically, spiritually and emotionally. Each and every day, I find it harder and harder to keep my sanity behind these walls. I wake up with you on my mind, and go to sleep with you on my mind. Real shit. I can't wait to feel you in my arms and smell the intoxicating scent of your perfume. You got me fiending, baby. I can't get enough of you. I'm obsessed, for real...

A big smile spread across Shirvetta's face as she read Heavy's letter and toyed with the icy, platinum nametag, bearing his name. Although she was a Thug Misses, she was still a lady at heart and a hopeless romantic. She loved everything that was looked at as cliché when it came to love, like flowers, cards, chocolates, diamonds, picnics and, last but not least, letters. No one knew this better than Heavy. That's why, every now and again, he chose to write to her instead of calling her.

I'd like to thank you for holding me and our family down in my absence. I know it isn't easy running this thing of ours, and I'd like to relieve you of some stress, by letting Golden handle things from here on out. I have one hundred percent faith in him, and have been grooming him since his stay here with me. If it wasn't for junior falling victim to dope and being so reckless, I would have let him oversee the family business. But a drug habit and responsibilities are a recipe for disaster. And we've worked entirely too hard to build what we have to watch it go up in smoke. So, with your blessings, I'd like to place Golden at the head of the table and let him conduct business on our behalf.

Love your sweet hubby,

Heavy

Shirvetta smiled like a teenage girl asked out by her crush. She folded the letter, placed it back in its envelope, kissed it and set it beside the tub on the floor. She picked up her cellphone and made a call. She played with the soapy foam as she listened to the phone ring.

***

"Babe, who is that?" Aries asked.

"Ma-dukes," Golden replied, looking at his cellular screen. Aries snuggled back beside him and closed her eyes. "What's up, ma?" He answered the call.

"Did I hit chu at a bad time?" Shirvetta replied.

"Nah. I'm just laid up witcho daughter-in-law. Why? What's up?"

Shirvetta took an exasperated breath. "Your father and I feel its best that you take things over, so I'm steppin' down as head of the business. From now on, I'll ride shotgun and back any plays you make. I must warn you though, son, a lot comes with holdin' this thing of ours down. You think you can handle it?"

Golden sat up in bed, slipping his arm around Aries's shoulders and kissing her on the forehead. "No doubt. I'm fully confident in handling the title that's being given to me. You and pop have given me alla the tools I need to succeed. My only concern is how yo' oldest is gon' feel about me taking up a position that's rightfully his. Nigga may feel like I'm stepping on his toes, especially with us bumpin' heads earlier today."

"Yeah. I know. That's why I called him before I called you, to see how he'd take it. Surprisingly, it went quite well. He's okay with you leading the family."

"For real?"

"I'd never lie to you, son. You got his blessing, so it's all a go." Golden smirked, hearing this. "As far as what went down between y'all this evening, I'm gonna need you to apologize to your brother."

"What? I wish I would. Ma, that muthafu—I mean, that nigga pulled a gun out on me. Two of 'em, as a matter of fact, and threatened to blow the kid's brains out."

"I know. He told me." Shirvetta told him. "He gave me the rundown. He also mentioned the reason behind him doing it. If it wasn't for the fact that you're his blood, I wouldn't blame 'em if he did slump yo' retarded ass."

"Ma, you taking his side?"

"Right is right and wrong is wrong, Golden. You said some pretty disrespectful shit to yo' brother, and I'm sure, if you weren't his sibling, he would have made you suffer the consequences of that slick mouth of yours. Dope-fiend or not, you're well aware of how your brother gives it up."

Golden nodded in agreement to what his mother had to say. She was speaking facts. He was out of line for coming at Cowboy the way he had, and he would have been deserving of whatever he got for the violation. Golden had never been a man too big to admit his wrongs and apologize. In this case, Cowboy was in the right, so he didn't have any problem with manning up and saying he was sorry to him.

"When you put it that way, ma, you're right. Soon as I get off the jack witchu, I'll hit up bruh and smooth thangz over."

"Good. 'Cause he made it clear he's not makin' this next move with us, unless you do just that, and like it or not, we need 'em on this one."

"Son, puttin' his foot down, huh? I can respect that."

"Anyway, I'ma letchu go so you can call your brother. I'ma finish washing up so I can get out this tub. I love you."

"I love you, too, ma." Golden disconnected the call and hit Cowboy up. His cellphone rang for what seemed like forever before he picked it up.

"Yeah?"

"Aye, look, I'ma get right to it," Golden began, as soon as he heard his brother's voice. "I apologize for the way I came at chu in front of that bodega earlier. What I said was mad disrespectful, and should have never been said, especially to someone I love." The line was silent. "Yo, Cow, you there?"

"Anythang for ma, huh?"

"You're right. Ma did holla at me. I wasn't with givin' you this call at first, but once I thought about it, you deserved an honest apology, B."

"You fuckin' right I do."

"You think you should apologize for pointing yo' blickies in my face?"

"My nigga, I don't know who you cop yo' dope from, but I need yo' plug 'cause that shit is awesome."

Golden grinned and shook his head. "Same ol' Cowboy."

"Sho' you right, tell the old lady I'm in. Peace." Cowboy disconnected the call.

Golden didn't waste any time shooting a text to Shirvetta to let her know Cowboy was down for the lick.

***

The next night...

Biggie, who was wearing a welding mask, was on his knees at the door of a safe, trying to cut it open with a focused-torch. Golden, who was also wearing a welding mask, stood on the opposite side of him, with his hands overlapping on top of a sledge hammer. He watched the sparks fly, while his younger brother was hard at work. He was hoping this lick would be an easy grab, but it was proving to be more difficult than they predicted.

Biggie turned off his torch, flipped up the shield of his mask and shot to his feet. In a fit of frustration, he smacked the side of the safe with his gloved hand.

"Fuuuuck, my nigga," Biggie shouted then wiped the sweat from his forehead.

Golden flipped up the shield of his mask. "What's up, bruh?"

"Man, I got the heat turned up to the max, but I still can't cut through this bitch. I think it's made outta Monel."

"Monel? Fuck is that?"

"A form of metal that's tougher than stainless steel. The only way we're gettin' in this bad boy is if fat ass gives us the combo. Otherwise, we can kiss the goodies in here goodbye."

"The only way is through the combo, huh?" Golden asked, walking around the safe, massaging his chin and thinking about the situation.

"Yep. And that chunky ass nigga is not gon' come off it."

"Oh, he will," Golden said as the torch in Biggie's hand caught his eye. He took it from him and examined it closely.

"How the hell do you figure that? We beat the dog shit outta dude, plus made examples outta his homies. Nigga still didn't crack."

"He will, after I get done with 'em." Golden smiled wickedly and fired up the torch.

Biggie smiled wickedly beside him. The youngster knew what his brother was leaning towards doing to their victim to get the safe's combination from him, and he was there for it.

***

"Cowboy, where the fuck you going?" Baby Girl asked, looking from him to the trap house.

"I gotta make a run real quick, sis. It's right around the corner," Cowboy told her. "I'll be right back. Trust me."

Baby Girl took him in from head to toe. He was showing all the signs of a fiend in need of their medication. "Nigga, this ain't the time for you to be getting high. Our family is…"

A vicious backhand across Baby Girl's face cut her short. Holding her stinging cheek, she looked at Cowboy like he'd lost his goddamn mind. Snarling, she pointed her gun at his face with every intention of pulling its trigger.

"Either you gon' squeeze that bitch or you not." Cowboy said, making a left at the corner of the residential street. "Makes no difference to me, but hurry up. I don't like guns in my face."

Baby Girl couldn't bring herself to clap her own brother, no matter how hard she tried. She took a few breaths to calm herself down, then she took the gun off him. "The next time you raise yo' hand to me, brother or not, I'ma blow yo' fuckin' head off."

"I copy that," Cowboy replied, without looking her way.

***

Cowboy pulled up on the D-Block he frequented and motioned over the dope-boy he was familiar with. He couldn't see it, but the little nigga was smiling when he saw him. The kid knew, any time Cowboy came through, he was going to buy at least fifty bucks worth of heroin. The dope-boy looked up and down the block before jogging across the street.

"What will it be, big homie?" the dope-boy asked.

"My usual, youngin', let's not start actin' brand new now." Cowboy replied, discreetly slipping him the folded up fifty dollar bill from his palm.

The dope-boy gave the block a scan for the presence of the law before pulling out five packets of ten dollar heroin tangled in a beige rubber band. Sneakily, he dropped the packets into Cowboy's lap and walked away without saying a word.

"Hold up, nigga, I know you not finna shoot that shit up right here." Baby Girl frowned, leaning up front. Cowboy had pulled out the carrying case he kept on him at all times and unzipped it. The case had everything he needed in order to prepare his fix.

"What's it look like?" Cowboy said, pulling the tourniquet tight around his arm with his teeth.

"Yo, we've gotta get back over there. Anything could be happening right now with ma and them," Baby Girl told him.

"Don't sweat it, lil' mama, ma and our brothers know how to handle them—them—" Cowboy's eyes narrowed as he pushed down on the plunger, feeding his hungry vein the dope it craved.

Chapter 6

"Y'all niggas know who the fuck I am, son? Y'all muthafuckaz know what mob I'm connected to? Huh?" Chris Stacks, wearing a mean mug, looked up at Shirvetta. His face was lumpy and his left eye was swollen shut.

Shirvetta used her gun to lift the saucer-size medallion lying on Chris Stack's chest and examined it. The piece was flooded with diamonds. It had a C and an S at its center, with a dollar sign between them.

"Me and my boys know exactly who you are. My crew doesn't make any moves without doing our homework first." Shirvetta replied, looking up from the medallion and into his furious eyes.

"Good. Then you know that once my people find out who you muthafuckaz are, you're gonna regret the day you decided to run up in my —"

Shirvetta cracked Christ Stack's across the bridge of his nose and blood gushed out of his nostrils. His eyes rolled back, and his head rolled around his shoulders. He blinked his eyes repeatedly, and tried his best to shake off his daze.

"Nigga, you're in no position to threaten me." Shirvetta scowled behind her mask and slowly mashed her boot against the crotch of his jeans.

Chris Stack's face balled up and a vein bulged at his temple. He gritted his teeth. His testicles felt like they were going to burst under so much pressure. Once Shirvetta felt like she'd gotten him in line, she lifted her boot from his nutsack and he sighed with relief.

"Whatever y'all fuck niggaz gon' do to the kid, do it." Chris Stacks told her fearlessly. "'Cause I'm not finna give y'all shit, you can kiss my rich ass. Fuck y'all." His face contorted into a mask of anger and he gave her the evil eye. He looked like a Rottweiler that couldn't wait to be set loose so he could maul an intruder. "You better kill me now, 'cause I swear to God, if I live through this, I'm comin' after each and every one of you bitchez with all I got." He spat a bloody loogie on Shirvetta's boot.

She looked at the glob with disgust, and then up at him. She was hot.

"Yo, son, I know you didn't just spit on my Ma-dukes. You got me and my bro fucked up, if you thank we gon' let chu disrespect our OG." Golden said as he emerged from the basement door. He was wearing the welding mask and carrying the focused-torch.

Biggie was coming up behind him with his gun at his side. He was scowling from behind his ski mask. He'd overheard the shit Chris Stack's was popping, just as Golden had. All of Shirvetta's children were overprotective of her, but Golden and Biggie were especially.

"Nigga, fuck you and this bitch." Chris Stacks harked up another glob and spat on Golden's welding mask.

Golden was infuriated. Even with his face being covered by the mask, Christ Stacks knew he'd gotten under his skin, and this made him laugh maniacally.

"Hahahahahahahahahaha." Chris Stacks threw his head back, shoulders rocking from laughter, tears peeking at the corner of his eyes.

"If you think that was funny, brace yourself for this next one. It's a real knee slapper. Ma, unzip this nigga's pants and pull out his meat." Golden fired up the torch. Chris Stacks' eyes bulged and he thrashed around in the raggedy wooden chair he was tied up in.

Shirvetta tucked her piece inside the holster under her arm. She unbuckled Chris Stacks' belt, unzipped his jeans, and reached inside his zipper for his penis.

"If I were you, big dawg, I'd tell us the combo to that safe before I got my dick melted like candle wax." Biggie suggested to Chris Stacks and folded his arms across his chest.

"You mean, y'all couldn't get the safe open?" Shirvetta asked, pulling Chris Stacks' joint out and standing back up.

Biggie shook his head. "Nah, ma. That sucka is too thick. I turned the torch up to the max and I still couldn't cut through it."

"Fight all you want, fat man, the only way you're gettin' outta this is tellin' us what we wanna know," Golden told Chris Stacks, as he continued to thrash around in the raggedy chair. Golden kneeled down in front of him and brought the focused-torch towards his dick and balls. Chris Stacks' eyes nearly popped out of their sockets when he felt the heat of the torch nearing his private parts.

"Okay, okay, okay. I'll tell you. I'll tell you the goddamn combo," Chris Stacks shouted. Sweat slid down his forehead and he swallowed the lump of fear in his throat.

"That's what I'm talkin' about, big bruh." Biggie shoved Golden in his back playfully.

"I told you we were gon' get them digits. A'ight, nigga, what's the mathematics?" Golden asked Chris Stacks.

"85-89-76-32." Chris Stacks spat out the combination.

"Appreciate it, big man," Golden patted him on his chubby cheek. He then turned to Biggie. "Yo, kid, I know you caught that, see if what's in that safe is worth our while."

Nodding, Biggie turned around to head down to the basement, tucking his stick at the small of his back.

Shirvetta noticed a wicked smile spread across Chris Stacks' lips as something caught his eye behind her. When she looked over her shoulder she saw a woman coming out of a trap door inside of the living room. Her eyes twinkled with murder as she gripped an M-16 assault rifle. She was laser-focused on Biggie, who she had every intention of killing. At that moment, everything appeared to move in slow motion. Shirvetta, gun in hand, hollered for Biggie to get down as she ran towards him. The woman that emerged from the trap door leveled her assault rifle at Biggie. Shirvetta flew across the kitchen and tackled her youngest son. Shots flew all around them, but one managed to graze Shirvetta's shoulder. Her face twisted in pain as she and Biggie collided with the floor.

Golden dropped the focused-torch and drew his piece from his waistband, turning to the active shooter. At the same time, Shirvetta rolled off of Biggie and pointed her gun at the shooter, who was trying to unjam her assault rifle. Together, Golden and Shirvetta fingered their triggers obsessively. Sparks flew and empty shell casings deflected off the floor. Little mama that came up from the trap door did the Dance of Death as she was lit up like a Christmas tree. Once Golden and Shirvetta's guns stopped spitting, homegirl dropped her M-16 and tumbled backwards down the staircase of the trap door, dramatically.

"Jamaiiiiiicaaaaaa," Chris Stacks hollered, after seeing his girlfriend gunned down. Tears burst out of his eyes and down his cheeks.

"You okay, baby boy?" Shirvetta asked Biggie, as she pulled him back up on his feet. He nodded yes. She hugged him into her and kissed him on the side of his mask.

"Ma, you gucci?" Golden asked with concern.

Shirvetta nodded. "Yeah. I'm alright."

Golden hugged her and she gave him a kiss on the cheek of his ski mask.

"I think that's the trap door Aries was talkin' about. If so, the work is stored there, beneath the fourth step. I'll check it out." Golden said before walking to the trap door.

"I'll be down in the basement, crackin' that safe," Biggie replied, disappearing through the basement door.

Shirvetta sat on Chris Stacks' lap and threw her arm around his shoulders. She watched as the tears flooded his cheeks and he stared ahead. She could tell that seeing his high school sweetheart offed fucked him up, but she didn't give a shit. If it was one thing she learned while in the jack game, it was that there wasn't any room for sympathy in it.

"Don't worry, sweetie, once you start hustlin' again, you can get up enough bread to buy you a new bitch." Shirvetta told him, wiping the tears from his cheeks with her finger, and then kissing him gently on his cheek.

Golden tucked his gun at the small of his back and kneeled down to the sixth step of the staircase of the trap door. He placed his ear on the fourth step, listened closely, and then knocked on it. A smile creased his lips when he realized this was the exact step he was looking for. He removed the welding mask and flung it aside. He withdrew a hunting knife, slid it into the slight opening of the fourth step and popped it open. As soon as he removed the lid, he encountered the two-hundred thousand dollars Aries had put him up on. It was separated in ten thousand dollar stacks by rubber bands and packaged in clear plastic. Golden removed the package of money, kissed it and tucked it under his arm. He walked back up the steps, sheathing his blade at his side.

"Jackpot," Golden announced as he emerged from the staircase, holding up the package of dead presidents.

"Well done, son." Shirvetta smiled, watching him stash the money inside his hoodie and zip it back up. She didn't know it, but Chris Stacks committed Golden's face to his memory, as well as the name Aries. He promised himself to make all of them pay for the suffering they caused that night.

Golden took his ski mask from his back pocket and pulled it down over his face. He walked over to his mother, fixing the eye-holes in it so he could properly see through them. A second later, Biggie was coming back through the basement door with a sack slung over his shoulder, looking like Santa Claus and shit.

"Ten pounds of that loud right here, big baby," Biggie smiled as he shook the contents of the sack, containing vacuumed bags of kush.

Shirvetta stood up, checking the time on her digital timepiece. "Well, we'd better be gettin' outta here before Jake surfaces. I know some of these ol' nosy ass neighbors have called them by now. Aaaaaaah." Shirvetta yawned and stretched her arms above her head, then twisted from side to side.

"Smooth. Lemme turn this nigga's lights out and we're ghosts," Biggie said, switching hands with the sack and drawing his stick. He casually walked over to Chris Stacks and placed his gun at his temple.

"Go ahead and kill a nigga, son. Do it. I don't give a fuck. I don't give a fuck," Chris Stacks hollered again and again.

Shirvetta glanced at the dead dope-boys they'd laid down upon bursting inside the house. They were sprawled on the carpet, with their guns lying within their reach. The poor bastards didn't stand a chance against the firepower they were packing, when they came through the door.

Shirvetta's thoughts then switched to his baby mama, Jamaica, who they'd just murdered. She knew Chris Stacks had three kids with her, and with her gone, the children only had him. Her being a mother had her feeling some type of way. She wouldn't walk out of that house with a peace of mind knowing she allowed Biggie to pop that nigga, Chris. For as long as she'd been putting it down in the streets, this was the first time she felt empathy for those she'd preyed upon.

"Stall 'em out, son." Shirvetta told Biggie, before he could send Chris Stacks to the afterlife.

"Ma, you sure? We don't want this situation comin' back to bite us in the ass. Think about it, queen." Biggie said, looking at his mother and waiting for her final decision.

While Biggie was looking at Shirvetta, she was staring at Chris Stacks, who was looking her right in her eyes. She thought about things really hard before delivering the verdict to her youngest boy.

"Let 'em breathe. Let's go," Shirvetta replied, walking out of the house behind Golden. Biggie tucked his piece and followed behind them.

As soon as they were out of sight, Chris Stacks thrashed around in his chair, like a raving lunatic. The chair squeaked louder and louder, until he eventually fell backwards in it. The rocking chair smashed into pieces upon hitting the kitchen floor. Chris Stacks scrambled to his sneakers and pulled off the rope. He ran over to the trap door and flipped on the light switch. When he looked at the bottom of the staircase, Jamaica was lying awkwardly in a pool of blood.

"Muthafuckaz," Chris Stacks shouted, and slammed his fist against the wall. He picked up the guns of the slain dope boys and ran out of the house.

Chapter 7

Shirvetta, Golden and Biggie spilled out of the house and onto the sidewalk. They looked up and down the block for the getaway van, but it wasn't anywhere to be found.

Where the fuck is this nigga Cowboy, man? As soon as that thought crossed Golden's mind, he heard screeching tires and saw the getaway van bending the corner at the end of the block. The van jerked to a stop in the middle of the street, with its sliding side door open. Golden and Shirvetta hopped inside the van, with Biggie coming up behind them. Biggie was about to hop in the van, when a bullet slammed into his back. He grimaced as he stumbled forward but caught his balance before he could fall. After the first bullet, several more followed, with rapid succession. The small block sounded like a war zone in Iraq.

"Biggie," Baby Girl called out from the driver's seat, having seen her brother shot. She came from behind the wheel with her piece and helped Shirvetta pull Biggie inside the van. Golden, enticed to get some get back, pulled out a second gun and jumped down into the street. Chris Stacks stood in the doorway of the house, talking tough and letting his sticks talk. Sparks flew as bullets ricocheted off the gate and punctured holes in the side of the getaway van.

Golden finger fucked the triggers of his guns, and bullets flew like a flock of pigeons. Chris Stacks' face balled up in agony, as he was riddled with slugs. He fired his guns aimlessly and tumbled down the steps, landing on his back.

He had a funny look in his eyes and his mouth moved awkwardly.

Ho-ass nigga, Golden thought as he lowered his smoking poles and spat on the curb. He tucked one of his warm guns in his waistband and climbed into the back of the van. "You good, lil' bruh?" he asked before pulling the door of the van shut.

Biggie nodded. "I'm a'ight. This vest saved me from becoming a quadriplegic." He lifted his hoodie and revealed the Kevlar bulletproof vest strapped underneath. Him and Golden exchanged smiles and dapped up.

"Where the fuck were you two?" Golden asked Baby Girl, after he snatched off his ski mask. He was angry and his face was sweaty.

Baby Girl adjusted the rearview mirror so she could see Cowboy in the back of the van. "Tell 'em where we were, Cowboy. Go on and tell 'em."

Cowboy was slumped against the wall of the van in a dope-fiend nod. Golden looked around at everyone and then back at him. His eyes were big and his mouth was hanging open. He couldn't believe his big brother had put all their lives at risk so he could get high.

"You son of a bitch," Golden roared, backhand slapping Cowboy. As soon as he collided with the floor of the van, Golden rushed over to him and unleashed a flurry of punches, hitting him in every exposed area of his body. Cowboy balled up, protecting his head and privates. He was all muscle and bracing himself so Golden's blows did little to hurt him.

"Bro, chill, chill." Biggie snatched Golden off their sibling. Golden tried his best to break his younger brother's hold, but he held fast.

"Golden, knock it off. The last thing we need is to get pulled over," Shirvetta said, sitting up against the opposite side of the van from Cowboy. He was looking around like he didn't know what the hell was going on.

"Fuck off me, Biggie." A seething Golden shoved his younger brother off him. He looked at Baby Girl and could see the bruising on her cheek. He narrowed his eyes, thinking they were playing tricks on him, and took a closer look. The area below her eye was swollen and bruised bluish-black. "Yo, tell me bruh didn't put his hands on you."

Baby Girl stole a glance at him.

"In this family, we don't snitch," Baby Girl replied, keeping her focus on the road ahead.

Golden's head twisted back around to Cowboy, on some exorcist shit. His eyebrows dipped and his nose wrinkled. The nigga looked like a full-blown psychopath. "Say, bruh, you got the game fucked up, if you think you gon' be puttin' yo' hands on any female in this family. I see you've gotten a lot bigga since I've been away. Well, I hope all them muscles gon' help you inna fade 'cause we fa sho' gon' rumble, when we get back." Golden slammed his fist into his palm continuously, like he was wearing a catcher's mitt.

Upon hearing Cowboy had put hands on his sister, Biggie stopped tending to his mother's wound and mad dogged him. He started to rush him, but then he thought about what his mother said about them getting pulled over.

Nah, this big ol' nigga need his ass beat, Biggie thought before going to make his move. He turned to do just that when his mother grabbed his arm. When he looked back at her, she shook her head no, and he relaxed.

"You think 'cause I'ma dope-fiend, you gotta easy win on yo' hands, lil nigga? You forgot I was pop's first pupil," Cowboy held up his fists. "I was throwin' these thangz when you were pissin' in ya Spiderman draws and checkin' under yo' bed for monsters."

"Yeah. I hear you, *gangsta*, but we gon' see if you walk it like you talk it." Golden told him.

"Indeed." Cowboy replied, sitting back against the wall of the van again. He picked up one of his twin revolvers and started spinning its cylinder. It was the only sound inside of the van, and when it stopped, he'd fall back into his dope-head nod again.

Golden nudged Biggie and whispered into his ear. "Soon as we get home, I need you to lure ma and Baby Girl away from the living room. I need you to keep 'em away for as long as it takes me to discipline Mr. Billy Badass here."

Biggie nodded understandingly.

The spinning of the revolver's cylinder started back up again. Golden and Biggie looked to where the sound was coming from and found Cowboy toying with his pistol. His head was tilted down and he was giving them the evil eye. They were pretty sure he'd heard their conversation.

***

Bwap, wop, wam.

Golden stumbled back from the three punch combination Cowboy gave him. He bumped up against the kitchen table, disturbing the vase full of flowers. Wiping his mouth, he looked to his hand and saw blood. The sight of it seemed to piss him off. Balling his fists, Golden charged at Cowboy, ready to get some get-back. He danced around on his feet, bobbing and weaving his older brother's next attack. He gave him a rib crushing right hander that made him moan like a wounded bear with its paw caught in a trap.

The brothers rumbled, ignoring the shouting and pounding at the bathroom door. Golden had gotten Biggie to lock Shirvetta and Baby Girl in the bathroom by propping a chair below the doorknob. Now Biggie was standing on the sidelines, watching him and Cowboy fight. He threw phantom punches, imagining it was him in the brawl.

"I hit hard, don't I, lil' bruh? Not bad for a no good dope-fiend, huh?" A sweaty Cowboy asked, after giving Golden a two piece. He had swelling under his eye and a busted lip. It had been a while since he'd put the beats on a nigga, and this fight with his little brother was a reminder of how rusty he was. Still, even as a junkie, he was more than capable of defending himself when the situation called for it.

Golden spat on the carpet and swallowed blood. He couldn't front, Cowboy could still throw hands. He may even be able to whip him. He refused to lose to a drug addict, though. That was something his ego couldn't handle.

Bop, wop, bam.

Cowboy stuck his ass three more times. Golden came at him again. He bobbed from side to side, dodging it, and came back with a fierce two piece. Golden stumbled backwards but caught himself. Cowboy rushed in to finish him, but everything he threw fell short. Golden saw an opening, and made him pay for it. A kidney shot brought Cowboy down to one knee. He sat there wincing and holding himself.

Unh huh. Talk that shit now, Billy Badass, Golden thought with a smirk on his lips and his fists at his sides. He walked around Cowboy, waiting for him to get up so they could lock ass again.

Boom, boom, boom, boom.

Shirvetta and Baby Girl continued banging at the bathroom door. Their screaming and shouting went ignored, just like the rest of the noise they made.

"Boy, if you weren't my blood, I'd do you something filthy right now. My word to God." Golden said, bumping his gloves together.

"Yeah, whatever, muthafucka." Cowboy slowly rose to his feet and got into a fighting stance. He kept his left arm at his side because his kidney was killing him. He'd have to contend with one fist now, but he didn't give a rat's ass. He wasn't about to pack it up and take it home. Fuck that. He wasn't just fighting to win, he was fighting for his siblings' respect.

"Tell you what, bruh, to keep things fair, I'ma use one arm, too," Golden said, holding his left arm behind his back. He saw that Cowboy was vulnerable and he didn't want an easy win. This was his way of evening the odds.

Cowboy nodded in a display of respect. Golden returned the gesture. The brothers moved around like professional boxers, looking for an opening to launch an attack. They threw a few jabs at each other. They connected but they weren't serious enough to do any real damage. Cowboy stayed locked in on Golden, working his jab. Golden bobbed and weaved the advance easily. But he and Biggie got the surprise of a lifetime when Cowboy brought his other fist into play. He gave him a left, right, body shot, and finished him with a right cross. Golden stumbled back fast and collided with the glass coffee table. The coffee table exploded and broken glass flew everywhere.

Biggie had a shocked look on his face, when he saw Golden come down on the coffee table. Golden struggled to get up, but he was dizzy and his legs felt like Jell-O. Cowboy stood over him with a devilish grin on his face. He'd managed to fool Golden into thinking he'd been seriously injured in order to get him to drop his guard. He knew it was fucked up to play his little brother like that, but the way he saw it, a win was a win.

Cowboy spat his black mouth-guard on the floor among the broken glass and splinters of the coffee table. As he pulled off his boxing gloves, the bathroom door blew open. Shirvetta and Baby Girl spilled out into the hallway, having tackled it open. Baby Girl scrambled to her sneakers and then helped her mother up. Together, they made their way inside of the living room, where Biggie was trying to help Golden up. Biggie was staring at Cowboy so intensely, they thought he'd melt like warm ice cream.

"Oh, my God, what happened?" Shirvetta asked, grabbing Golden's other arm to help him up.

"Ain't nothing. Just hadda spank the lil nigga to remind 'em who big bruh is," Cowboy said, picking up his revolvers and sliding them in their holsters one by one.

"You a foul ass nigga Cowboy, you ain't have to play bruh like that. We're family," Biggie said. He stretched Golden's arm over his shoulders, while Baby Girl took his other arm from their mother and did the same.

"Whatever, homeboy, there's more where that came from, if you want some," Cowboy told him. He figured, if he could park Golden on his ass, then Biggie would most definitely prove to be light work.

Chapter 8

"Y'all take y'all brother into my bedroom, while I grab the first aid kit to clean 'em up." Shirvetta told Biggie and Baby Girl.

Biggie was so focused on Cowboy, he didn't hear a word his mother said. In fact, he didn't hear his sister, who was calling his name, either. He was entirely too busy weighing his options. He really wanted to test the waters and catch Cowboy's fade. His heart was telling him to go for it, while his brain was telling him otherwise. Although Heavy had taught all of his children how to fight, except for Biggie, he could never quite get the hang of it, so he gave up and picked up the great equalizer, a gun. Once he saw how niggas reacted when he upped that hammer, he didn't bother learning how to properly fight. He didn't see any use for it, when he could just blast whomever he had a problem with.

Biggie understood that, if he rumbled with Cowboy, he'd come out on the losing end. There wasn't any doubt in his mind of that. With this knowledge, he decided it was best to let him have this W and catch him on the rebound, in the near future.

"Biggie," Baby Girl shouted.

"My bad. What's up, sis?" Biggie snapped out of it.

"Boy, where the hell did you just go? Momma wants us to help Golden into her bedroom, while she gets the first aid kit."

"My fault. I'm tripping. Come on," Biggie said, helping her along with Golden. He glanced at Cowboy, who was smirking at him, while adjusting his pistols in their holsters.

"Pussy-ass nigga," Biggie said under his breath.

"Yeah. That's what the fuck I thought, lil nigga. This ain't what chu want," Cowboy replied. He grabbed the duffle bag of the trap money they'd stolen and then took the money counter from underneath the kitchen cabinet. He sat down at the kitchen table and placed the items in front of him.

"And just what the hell do you think you're doing, Mr. Man?" Shirvetta asked, with the yellow first aid kit tucked under her arm.

"I'm 'bouta count up this bread, set my cut aside and then I'm raisin' up outta here 'fore I have to get in yo' other son's ass." Cowboy told her, scratching underneath his chin. He was due for a dose of his medication, but he'd have to fight off the hunger, until he got his ends from the latest lick.

"Cowboy, you're my oldest. I love you to death, but I don't trust you around nan dollar," Shirvetta admitted. "After I take care of Golden, we'll all sit at the table and divvy up the spoils. Got it?"

"Yeah. I got it. Now mosey along, I can't keep these demons waiting," Cowboy told her, as he scratched the inside of his arm. The demons he spoke of were the ones whispering in his ear about how they were in dire need of dope.

Shirvetta shook her head and walked down the hall.

***

Illmatic was lit like it was the night the ball was supposed to drop in Times Square. The club was packed from wall to wall with people drinking, smoking, bumping and grinding. The blue disco balls, hanging from the ceiling, spun around, creating a lightshow for all the party goers. The walls pulsated from the loud music. The atmosphere was so humid sweat was sliding down the walls, and people were perspiring.

Tonight wasn't your typical club night. Tonight was special, and it would most definitely be one to remember. Rich Loc, the nigga who was celebrating his birthday at Illmatic, girlfriend had saw to that. Rich Loc was on the dance floor, with a gold bottle of Ace of Spades, Crip walking to Bad Azz's *Wrong Idea*. The audience he'd drawn stared at him in amazement. Some of them cheered him on, while others filmed him on their cellular phones.

Rich Loc's face and chest were sweaty. He shone under the blue lights of the spinning disco balls. He had a royal blue bandana tied around his head, a blue chinchilla vest over his bare body, and two million dollars in icy gold jewelry around his neck and wrists. Now, at first glance of Rich Loc, one wouldn't think he was as deep in the streets as he was. His appearance gave you superstar basketball player vibes. He was six-foot-two, slender, yet cut, with tattoos galore on his milk chocolate skin. He had a fifteen hundred dollar taper fade, and his facial hair was trimmed into a remarkable goatee.

Rich Loc started his love affair with the streets at the tender age of eleven, running G-packs for a local czar named Big Guap. When Guap caught a bid with the feds for drug trafficking, in his absence, Rich Loc formed his own squad of money hungry savages, and picked up where he left off. His networking landed him ties to the Los Zetas Cartel, whose bosses were willing to hit him with stupid bricks. From there, the Dope God had his Unholy Angels pumping his poison in the ghettos of New York, turning the very streets he'd run as a snot nosed kid into badlands.

Rich Loc passed his champagne bottle to his lady, Gabby, who was egging him on from the sidelines. He really went in on the Crip walk then. Snatching off his bandana, he wiped the sweat from his forehead and hit a few more moves. He motioned Gabby over, but she shook her head, no. The audience nudged her forward and urged her to step on the dance floor. Rich Loc took the bottle from her, drank some and then led her to the floor. They performed an act, doing the Crip walk together. He then stepped back, guzzling the champagne, and excitedly watching his girl do his dance.

Once Gabby had finished dancing, the audience cheered her on and pumped their fists. Rich Loc, using his bandana, patted Gabby's sweaty forehead dry and poured her a mouthful of bubbly. Holding hands, Rich Loc and his First Lady bowed, then retreated towards the Very Important Persons section with his army of killers in tow. The audience Rich Loc and Gabby had drawn, applauded their performance as they walked away. The song was then replaced with Usher's *Super Star*.

Homie posted outside the velvet rope that sectioned off the V.I.P section, unhooked the rope and stepped aside, so Rich Loc and his entourage could walk through. He hooked the rope back, once everyone had passed, smoothened out his tie, and continued to hold down his post.

Gabby sat down on the black leather couch with a silver platter of various fruits and patted her lap. Rich Loc downed what was left of the champagne, belched and sat the gold bottle on the table. He stretched out on the couch and laid his head in Gabby's lap. She caressed the side of his face, while smiling down at him. He smiled back up at her. They kissed slowly and passionately.

"A nigga crazy about cho ass, shorty. That's my word," Rich Loc swore.

"You better be 'cause I'm even crazier about you," Gabby replied with a smirk.

"Real shit. I love you, ma," he told her, wearing a serious expression. "I'd kill and I'd die behind you, on everythang I love."

"I love you, too, pa," she told him, kissing him again, and then feeding him red grapes, like he was a king or some shit.

The hostess, a pretty, slender, twenty-year-old, light-skinned Black girl, rocking a blonde fade and diamond nose piercing, entered the V.I.P section. She was dressed in a white button-down, black bowtie, and black slacks. She placed all the empty flutes and champagne bottles upon her tray. She turned around to walk away, but Rich Loc called her back. Still munching on the grapes, he unzipped the colorful Gucci pouch attached to the loops of his jeans and pulled out an obscene amount of dead presidents. He counted out three thousand dollars and tossed it on the tray.

"Yo, foe mo' of them gold bottles, ma. The rest of that is all you," Rich Loc told her, before he was fed another grape. The hostess thanked him with a smile and made her way out of the V.I.P section.

Rich Loc settled his head back in Gabby's lap, as he continued to munch on the delicious grapes. She fed him another one and kissed him again. They started making out, when his cellular phone rang. He ignored it at first, but it kept ringing, so he decided to see who it was.

"Mmmm, hold on, babe, lemme see who this is," Rich Loc told her, before taking out his cellphone. When he glanced at the screen, he balled up his face, wondering who was calling him from Mount Sinai Hospital. He answered the call and sat up beside Gabby.

She frowned, staring at him, wondering what was going on.

"Pa, what's the matter?" Gabby asked.

Rich Loc threw up his hand so she'd give him a minute to see what was going on. He listened intently at what he was being told before hopping up on his two thousand dollar designer sneakers and disconnecting the call.

"We've gotta go," Rich Loc told Gabby, as he pulled her up on her red bottom heels. He then looked to his killers who were drinking, smoking and mingling with a few females. "Y'all niggaz come on, cuz, we gotta go."

"What's the deal, cuz?" one of the killers asked. He was sitting on the couch on the opposite side of the section with a five-foot-two, caramel thang in his lap. He'd planned on taking her home to try the new sex positions he saw Wesley Pipe's do in a porn flick the other night.

"I'll explain everythang onna way, but we've gotta go now. I'll meet chu niggaz at the truck," Rich Loc told him, hurrying out of the V.I.P section and dragging Gabby along.

Trotting alongside him in her heels, she damn near fell, so she made him stop so she could remove her shoes. She took her shoes into her other hand and took hold of his with her other. Together, they bumped their way past everyone dancing and talking around them.

"Bae, are you gon' tell me what happened?" Gabby asked, trying her best to keep up with him.

"My brother," He replied with a scowl.

"You mean, Chris?"

"Yeah. Stacks. He's been shot."

***

Mount Sinai Hospital

Rich Loc ran down the hallway, with Gabby on his heels. A nurse tried to stop them, but they ignored her. Their only concern was how bad off his brother was. Rich Loc stopped in the doorway, breathing hard, with Gabby by his side. His brother's head was wrapped in bandages, and so was his torso. In fact, the blood from his gunshot wounds had begun to saturate the bandages wrapped around his torso. A see-through oxygen mask covered his nose and mouth. He had tubes running in and out of his body, and there was medical machinery beside his bed to monitor his vitals. While most would have seen a grown man laid up in the hospital bed on the brink of death, Rich Loc saw the nine-year-old kid that used to follow him and his friends around, begging to be a part of whatever mischief they had planned for the day.

"Damn, lil bro," a teary-eyed Rich Loc uttered, voice cracking emotionally. He took a step forward and nearly fell.

Luckily, Gabby caught him, before he could meet the linoleum. "It's okay, babe, I got it." Gabby nodded and released his arm.

Rich Loc walked to Chris Stack's beside on wobbly legs and a tear soaked face. He pulled up a chair and took his meaty hand into both of his. He caressed his hand with one hand, and wiped his dripping eyes with the other.

"Stacks, son, I don't know who did this to you, but I'll promise you this, I'm gonna make it my life's mission to find out," Rich Loc swore, glassy-eyed. "And when I do, my right hand to God, I'm gonna crush all parties involved. That's my word, and my word is bond." He pressed his forehead to Chris Stack's hand and cried his eyes out.

The scene touched Gabby's heart so much that she began crying. She snatched a few tissues from the Kleenex box on the nightstand and dabbed her eyes dry. Gabby wrapped her arms around him from behind and kissed him on the side of his face. She could literally feel his body trembling as he wept, and it was unusual to her. In all of her years of knowing him, she'd never seen him shed a tear, until now.

"I gotcho back, bae. We're gon' get these niggaz that touched bruh-in-law. Just tell me what chu need me to do, and it's done." Gabby assured him, kissing him on the back of the head and neck. Closing her eyes, she laid the side of her face against the back of his head and held him tighter.

Rich Loc dabbed his eyes with a blue bandana and blew his nose. He pulled himself together as best as he could and cleared his throat. He craned his head over his shoulder so he could look at Gabby's face. She was startled when she saw his glassy, red-webbed eyes and wrinkled forehead. He didn't know it, but he looked every bit of a psychopath to her.

"I'm glad you said that, baby," Rich Loc said, kissing the side of her hand. "'Cause right now, I want you to holla at

Parelli for me. You tell 'em to put the word out that I gotta hunnit racks for anyone that can finger the fools who did this to Stacks. Can you do that?"

"It's already done, beloved," Gabby assured him, kissing his forehead and then his lips. Pulling out her cellular phone, she walked out of the room and left Rich Loc at his brother's bedside.

Chapter 9

Golden walked through the door and flipped on the living room's light switch. He carried the knapsack containing his cut from the lick into the kitchen and grabbed a Heineken out of the refrigerator. He held the cold bottle against his bruised cheek as he headed towards his bedroom.

"Old bitch-ass nigga, he def gon' have to run that shit back." Golden thought aloud, twisting the cap off his beer with his teeth, and taking a drink. He walked into his bedroom and stashed his loot inside the safe in his closet's floor. When he laid the flap of carpet back over the safe, he felt his cellphone vibrate with a text message. Closing the closet door behind him, he looked at his phone's screen and saw it was Aries that had hit him up.

Aries: *Bae, u good?* Translation: Did the lick go as planned?

Golden: *Somewhat.* Translation: We got what we came for but niggas winded up dead.

Golden and Aries spoke in a code that only they could decipher. Golden learned that Chris survived the bullets he'd put into him and was clinging to life in the hospital. He was also informed that Rich Loc was hot and heartbroken over Chris Stacks, and had ordered Aries to put the word out that he had a big bag for anyone that could tell him the whereabouts of his assailants.

Golden: *I drank the last of yo Moet. I'll have 2 buy u some mo.*

***

Golden's last text message made Aries feel like she was going to throw up. She doubled over, holding her stomach and pressing her hand against the vending machine. Her vision became obscured as tears filled her eyes. She began breathing like a pregnant lady in labor. That text meant Jamaica had been killed during the robbery. Aries felt like it was her fault that she was dead, because she was the one that had put the Loves onto the lick. If she wouldn't have told them about the goods Chris Stacks stashed, homegirl would still be alive.

Aries felt her cellphone vibrate with another text so she looked at it.

Golden: *My bad, ma. U forgive a nigga?*

Sniffling, Aries wiped her teary eyes and hit him back.

Aries: *Yeah. I forgive u. Gotta go. I luv u.*

Golden: *I luv u 2.*

Aries deleted the text conversation. She nearly jumped through the roof when she saw Rich Loc's reflection through the vending machine's window. She turned around to him, holding her hand to her chest.

"Sweet Jesus, baby, you scared the shit outta me," Aries told him.

"My bad, lil mama, I just came to check on you. You've been gone for a minute," Rich Loc kissed her on the cheek as he leaned down to grab the Pepsi out of the vending machine slot. He cracked it open and took a drink. Then he passed it to her. As she drank the soda he noticed her pink, glassy-eyes. His forehead wrinkled as he swept her hair out of her face and caressed her cheek. "I see you've taken baby bruh's situation hard. Me being in my feelings about 'em made me forget you had love for my nigga, too. My bad. Come here, yo."

Rich Loc hugged Aries into him and comforted her. She stared vacantly over his shoulder as tears flooded her cheeks. Her tears weren't for Chris Stacks at all, but she wouldn't dare tell Rich Loc this. Truthfully, she didn't really care for homie like that. The love in her heart was for Jamaica. The girl had become like a little sister to her. They told each other nearly everything. In fact, it was Jamaica who told her about the $200,000 in cash her baby daddy kept stashed in a step, behind a trap door, as well as the ten pounds of OG kush he'd stored inside the safe in the basement.

Goddamn, Jamaica, this one hit differently, you were my girl. Fuck, Aries thought. She closed her eyes and tears jetted down her cheeks.

***

Rich Loc and Aries kissed as they assisted each other getting undressed. Rich Loc held both of Aries's hands against the wall above her head. First, he kissed her again, sucked on her bottom lip and gently pulled it. Second, he bit the soft flesh underneath her chin, sucked on it and planted a trail of kisses down her chest. He grasped her perfectly round breasts and mashed them together. Gently, he pulled on her pointy nipples with his teeth, flicked and then sucked on them.

Aries held both sides of Rich Loc's head as he kissed his way down her flat stomach and over her diamond-stud navel piercing. He placed a leg over each of his shoulders and lifted her high against the wall. She placed her palms against the ceiling to keep from bumping her head. She gasped, feeling him run his tongue up and down her slit. He trapped her clit between his lips and flicked his tongue across it rapidly. Her eyes narrowed to their whites, and she bit down on her bottom lip. Her legs trembled. Her toes balled up. She squirmed and whined, listening to him manipulate her jewel.

"Ooooooooooh." Aries pressed her head back against the wall, licked her lips and humped into his mouth. The sounds of him munching on her lady parts drove her crazy and made her just that much wetter. "Baby, lemme—I wanna—I wanna suck yo' dick so—so fuckin' bad right now. Mmmmm," Aries stammered.

Rich Loc toyed with Aries clitoris a while longer before lifting her butt up and parting her cheeks. Her asshole was darker than her complexion, and winking like a flirtatious eye. Aries rubbed her clit in a circular motion, she held Rich Loc's gaze, while he ate her booty hole.

"Oh my God. Oh my fuckin' God, Rich. I'm about to—I'm 'bout to exploooode. Unh, unh, unh," Aries screamed like the fat white lady at the opera, jerking violently and saturating Rich Loc's mouth with her womanly juices. Tremors racked her body as he licked up her nectar like a thirsty kitten. He lowered her to her feet and her legs buckled like she was trying to stand up from a knockout. She grabbed hold of him, licking her juices from his face and glistening goatee. She then cupped his face, gave him a lust-filled kiss and sucked on his tongue.

"Suck my dick," Rich Loc told her.

"Nigga, I ain't suckin' jack shit with you telling me like that," Aries replied.

Rich Loc yanked her into him by her head, which had her looking at him from an awkward angle. He spoke to her with authority, real thuggish-like, "Bitch, get on yo' knees and suck a boss nigga dick, like I told you to." He barked as he pumped his piece, making it grow and harden. He shoved her back up against the wall and backhand slapped her. She looked at him hungrily, licking the trickle of blood from her mouth and biting down on her bottom lip. His roughing her up made her nipples stiffen and her clitoris stick out.

"Yes, daddy," Aries replied, rubbing her nipples with one hand and fingering her love-button with the other.

Rich Loc grabbed her by the neck, gave her a squeeze and kissed her deeply. He then lowered her down to her knees with one hand and rubbed his pipe back and forth across her full lips. He stuffed himself into of her mouth, making her cheeks balloon and her eyes tear. He held her hair in one fist, and held the other behind his back. They held eye contact as he fucked her mouth, causing hot saliva to run down his shaft and hang from his ball sack.

"Aaag, aaag, gag, gag, ack, ack," Aries gagged and choked on the end of his piece. The entire time she was fingering herself, making her twat squirt and form a small puddle on the floor.

"Oh, yeah. Yeah, boo. I love me a nasty ass ho. This the kinda shit thata make the loc bust all in yo' pussy and yo' mouth. Unh, unh. Yeah, yeah, bitch. Get it, get it," Rich Loc egged on with his head back, humping into her mouth. The combination of choking, gagging and sloshing of spit had him on the verge of bursting like a Glock with a switch.

"Cum for me, daddy—cum for mamas—ack, gack, hack," Aries choked as he pumped inside of her warm, wet mouth.

"Umm, umm, mmm." Rich Loc grunted while fucking her mouth recklessly. "Fuck, ma. Onna set, yo' shit alla that, but I want some of that pussy 'fore I bust this nut. I want chu onna floor, on yo stomach witcho cheeks spread."

Rich Loc popped his piece out of Aries' mouth. She wiped her wet lips and did like he'd instructed her. He straddled her from behind, pumping his meat until he saw clear cum oozing out of its pee hole. Aries held her butt cheeks apart, giving him another peek at her asshole. He sucked on his thumb and sunk it in her butt. She whimpered. He pressed his dick-head at the entrance of her tunnel and slid himself inside. He shuddered, feeling her hot, juicy insides. Her coochie felt like heaven to him, and at that moment, there wasn't anywhere else he'd rather be.

"Damn, bae, you, you stretching my pussy wide open, damn," Aries whined, digging her fingers into the carpeted floor. Her eyes were closed and her mouth was hanging open. While Rich Loc's left hand was latched onto her shoulder, the right one had its thumb in her ass to the knuckle. He was working himself in and out of her slowly, gradually building up speed. His eyes were closed like hers. They were in sync with his rhythm and riding the wave of his thug passion.

Rich Loc started fucking Aries savagely. He was clapping her cheeks so hard that ripples swept up her buttocks. Sweat bubbled out of his pores, cascaded down his body and dripped on hers. She called out his name, over and over again, which made him lay into her harder and faster.

"Rich, Riicch. Oh, Riiiich. Fuck me, fuck me, fuck." Aries's eyes turned white and her mouth hung open. Rich Loc was fucking the sound out her sexy ass.

"You gon' have my baby? Huh? You gon' gimme my prince, ma?" Rich Loc questioned her, while he piped her out like the cock-smith that he was.

"Yes, Rich, I'ma give you a son. I'ma have yo' baby. I'ma give you a lil prince," Aries swore. Her body jerked up and down as she was pumped full of dick.

"That's right, queen. You gon' give yo' king a, a, a prince. Unh, unh, unh," Rich Loc grunted with tightened jaws. He humped into her four more times, emptying his sack inside of her womb. Rich Loc, sweaty and hot, collapsed on top of Aries, breathing hard with his eyes closed. Aries smiled, loving the feeling of his body pressed against hers and his hot breath against the side of her neck.

"Mmmmm. That was great," Aries told him, pulling his arm around and kissing his vein-riddled hand.

"Fuckin' amazing, baby." Rich Loc replied, kissing her back and shoulder tenderly. He lay on top of her a while longer before getting up and pulling her to her feet. He led her into the master bedroom, where they smashed again.

***

Rich Loc lay in bed, smoking a blunt, with smoke moving around him like some sort of paranormal activity. There was a little less than half of the bleezy left, thanks to his negligence. He allowed Aries to partake in his vice but he winded up hogging it. It wasn't his fault. He'd heard stories about how good that California bud was but he didn't expect it to be hitting like this.

"Yo, I need you to keep it a stack wit a nigga." Rich Loc mashed what was left of the blunt in an ashtray and sat it back on the nightstand.

"I'm yo' ride or die. I'ma always keep it a thousand witchu, baby." Aries kissed him on his right pec and sat up in bed, propping her hand against the side of her head.

"Do you love a nigga? I mean, like, really, really love a nigga?" Rich Loc asked, looking into her eyes.

"Without question, I love you. Shit, you know that, especially after all the bullshit we've been through together."

"I hear you, ma, but I needa know how much?" He tucked her hair behind her ear and caressed her cheek.

"Lemme put it to you like this, if I hadda choose between hurtin' you or myself, I'd choose me every time," Aries swore. "I'd rather die than live the rest of my life without chu, Rich."

"Straight up?"

"Straight up."

Rich Loc lifted her chin up and kissed her, slipping her a little tongue at a time. "I love you."

"I love you, too."

"I'ma hop in this shower and get right. Don't keep a loc waiting," Rich Loc threw off the sheet and slid out of bed. Aries watched as he walked to the bathroom butt naked.

"I'll be there inna second, boo." Aries laid back on the bed, staring up at the ceiling with thoughts running through her mind. Right then, it suddenly hit her.

Bitch, you fucked up. You fucked up big time. Hell, you let cho self fall for both of them? Damn. Now what am I gonna do? Aries' brows wrinkled and she shook her head.

"Yo, ma, hurry up 'fore the water gets cold," Rich Loc called out from the bathroom.

"I'm coming, sweetie," Aries blew out smoke as she smashed the blunt out in the ashtray. She threw off the sheet and slid out of bed. She sauntered across the bedroom with her butt cheeks jiggling.

I'ma eventually have to choose between the men I love. I just hope, when the time comes, I make the right choice.

Chapter 10

"So, what's up? You love this nigga or what?" Golden asked.

"No, no, I don't love him. Baby, I swear to God, I was just fuckin' with him to survive out here, and make sure you were taken care of, while you were inside," Aries reasoned. She tried to embrace him but he shoved her. She broke down crying. She wasn't used to him acting in this manner. "I don't understand why you're acting this way. You gave me the okay to fuck with whatever nigga I needed to, since you were gonna be gone for five years, just as long as I didn't fuck with nobody you knew and I made sure you were good."

Golden couldn't front on shorty. He'd told her that, but now he was in a jealous rage. And he couldn't shake the images of that nigga Rich fucking his bitch from his mind's eye. He compared himself to the drug lord in every way imaginable. He was taller than him, stronger than him, had more money than him, and he definitely had more jewelry and assets. There was only one thing he didn't know for sure that was eating away at him. He knew he shouldn't ask but he just couldn't help himself.

"Yo, shorty, keep it one hunnit with a nigga, and don't lie either 'cause I know yo' ass."

"What is it, baby? What is it that chu wanna know?"

"Is his dick bigga than mine? I mean, keep it a stack." Golden said, pulling out his dick and letting it hang freely. It was thick and had veins running up and down it. "I needa know if he was laying the pipe down betta than me."

"Oh my fuckin' God, Golden, you can't really expect me to answer that."

"I knew it, bro. I fuckin' knew it," Golden shouted, with his hands on either side of his head, pacing back and forth. "This nigga rich ass fuck, and on top of that, his dick bigger than mine? Aww, fuck. I think I'm gonna be sick." He doubled over, holding his stomach. His cheeks swelled and he threw up.

"What? Golden, I never said that. What's the matter witchu?"

"You're right. You didn't say yes, but you didn't say no, either."

"Golden, your dick is bigger and your sex is better than his."

"You—you really mean that?" Golden looked at her, wiping the drool from the corner of his mouth.

"Of course, I do, baby. Come here." Aries said, opening her arms for a hug.

"See, cuz? I told you this bitch wasn't shit," a voice came from the doorway. When Aries turned around, an angry Rich Loc stepped into the bedroom with a gun at his side. Right then, Golden stood upright with his piece at his side, and what he'd eaten earlier on his shirt.

"I can't front, Rich. I've known this triflin' whore longer than you, but you know her better than I do." Golden's face balled up with animosity and he pointed his gun at Aries.

Aries' eyes widened and she threw up her hands. "Golden, wait, I love you."

Aries saw Rich Loc moving from the corner of her eye, and she turned to him. His face was balled up as well, and he was pointing his piece at her, too.

"Told the loc the same thang, so which of us is it that chu love, shorty? 'Cause it can't be the both of us." Rich Loc's nostrils flared.

"That's what I'm sayin'." Golden chimed in.

Aries was stuck. She didn't know what to say. She looked back and forth between both of her lovers. "I—I—I—"

"Dawg, fuck this lyin' ass bitch," Golden shouted and finger fucked his trigger rapidly.

Aries swallowed his first bullet, while the second one got her just below the chin. Rich Loc started firing right after Golden, striking her in the chest. As soon as she collided with the floor, both men walked up on her, shooting with what seemed like unlimited ammo, watching her body dance with each bullet it absorbed.

***

"Aaaaaaaaaaaaaaah." Aries shot up in bed, sweaty and screaming. Rich Loc woke up right after her, grabbing his strap from underneath his pillow and looking for burglars. He calmed down when he realized Aries just had a bad dream.

"It's okay, ma. It was just a bad dream. Come here," Rich Loc said, throwing his arm around her shoulders. She fell into his arms and cried into his chest. Still holding his piece, he rubbed her back to comfort her. "It's gonna be a'ight. I got chu. I gotchu forever." He kissed the top of her head.

Once Aries had calmed down that night, Rich Loc questioned her about her nightmare. She lied to him for fear of how he would react. She gave him some line of bullshit about a maniac in a hockey mask chasing her with a machete. He laughed and teased her about watching horror movies before bed, but she didn't trip. It was better than telling him the truth and winding up like she did in her dream.

***

A royal blue bandana print Lamborghini Sián zipped in and out of lanes, cutting in between cars, until it found an empty lane all to itself. The Italian sports car punched out, with its engine roaring like an untamed beast. It floated through traffic, like it was sitting on top of a cloud, hogging up the road. The driver pressed a button, and it transformed into a convertible, revealing its passengers, Rich Loc and Aries.

Aries had the biggest smile on her lips, as she stared at the icy platinum engagement ring decorating her finger. She could see a dozen of her reflections in the diamonds of her 8-karat ring. She and Rich Loc had just left a romantic boat ride, where he popped the question to her, while a violinist serenaded the beautiful moment. The way things had unfolded was out of a movie and she couldn't be happier.

Rich Loc's eyes were hidden behind a pair of designer shades. The tail ends of his blue bandana danced as the wind blew against him. He wore a solemn expression, while listening to Nipsey Hussle's *Victory Lap* and speeding like a NASCAR driver. He jerked to a stop at a red traffic light, grasped Aries' hand and kissed it. She cupped his face and kissed him. She could literally feel the butterflies in her stomach and her heart swelling with all of the love she had for him. It was just too bad all that shit was about to come to an end, in a matter of seconds.

Urrrrrrrrk!

Urrrrrrrrk!

A black van halted at the back of the Lamborghini and another one halted in front of it. A masked gunman hopped out of each van and upped a chopper on Rich Loc. He was about to grab the stick he kept underneath the driver's seat, when he felt an assault rifle to the side of his dome. He carefully lifted his hands up.

"I wish you would, you fake-ass Tupac, I'll blow yo' brains into that bitch's lap sittin' beside you," the masked gunman threatened, seeing Rich Loc reach for his gun. "Now turn that bullshit off, now."

Rich Loc kept one hand up, while using the other to turn the volume of his stereo down.

"Aaaaaaaah," Aries screamed loud enough for God Almighty to hear her. Another masked gunman yanked her out of the passenger seat by her hair. She lost one of her Red Bottom pumps in the process.

"Bitch, shut the fuck up 'fore I clap yo' ass out here. Get up, get cho ass up and get in the van." The masked gunman pulled Aries up roughly by her arm and shoved her from behind. She continued walking towards the van, with the masked gunman holding her at gunpoint. A third masked gunman snatched her inside of the van where he bound her wrists and gagged her mouth.

"My nigga, you know who the fuck you pullin' a jux on?" Rich Loc asked with a scowl. If looks could kill, the masked gunman would be lying dead in the intersection.

"I know exactly who you are, my guy. I also don't give a fuck," the masked gunman told Rich Loc, before slipping off his designer shades and placing them on his face. He then slipped the icy gold R.L choker from around his neck and pocketed it. "Now, get cho rich, flashy-ass outta the car."

Rich Loc lifted up the door and hopped out of the sports car. The masked gunman held him at gunpoint, while another one appeared out of nowhere. He was holding a piece with a silencer on its barrel. Rich Loc tensed up, thinking he was about to split his wig, but he walked right past him. He hopped behind the wheel of the Lambo, pulled the driver's door down and zipped away into the night. Once he'd put enough distance between him and the location of the lick, he sat his piece in his lap and snatched off his ski mask. Biggie tossed the ski mask onto the passenger seat and glanced up at the rearview mirror. He smirked, thinking of how smooth the lick had gone so far.

The masked gunman that had Rich Loc held at gunpoint, gagged him and bound his wrists. Pressing his chopper into his back, he ordered Rich Loc into the back of the van Aries was forced into and closed the door behind him. As he retreated to the van he'd come in, the van with Rich Loc and Aries as passengers drove away in a hurry.

***

"A'ight, homeboy, we're gonna skip the foreplay and get right to it. Where's the money and the dope?" Golden asked from behind the ski mask, pressing the chopper against Rich Loc's cheek.

Rich Loc gave him a death stare, refusing to utter a word.

Golden looked at him like he was crazy for challenging him. He flipped the assault rifle over in his hands and slammed it into his stomach. Rich Loc made a pained groan as he lifted his head back up. The wind had just been knocked out of him and he found it difficult to breathe. Golden snatched the duct tape from his lips and removed the sock from his mouth. "You wanna talk now?"

Rich Loc took the time to gather himself and shot Golden another death stare. Golden gave him a nod that let him know he respected his G. He knew Rich Loc wasn't going to tell him what he wanted to know. He rather die than come up off anything that would benefit a couple thieving ass niggas. The only way to get a nigga like him to cooperate was to threaten to harm someone they loved. Golden could think of one thousand things a man loved, but the top two were money and women.

Golden's eyes shifted to Aries, who was shuddering and crying in the corner of the van. A smile stretched across his lips. Rich Loc's eyes widened with fear off Golden's expression. That expression was all too familiar to him. He knew exactly what Golden had in store, if he didn't give him what he wanted, and it made his stomach turn.

Rich Loc's eyes followed Golden as he approached the corner of the van, where Aries was slumped. Golden snatched off Aries' black hood and kneeled to her. He swept her hair out of her face and caressed her cheek. Trembling, she looked up at him with snot sliding out of her nose and over the strip of tape covering her mouth.

"A nigga can't front, Richie Boy, you've got good taste. Realllll good taste," Golden said, feasting his eyes on Aries's luscious boobs and shapely figure. Licking his top row of teeth, he smiled devilishly and allowed his AK-47 to travel down her neck and into her cleavage. Seeing how traumatized Aries was from Golden's taunting, Rich Loc jumped to his feet and charged at him. Golden sidestepped him and whacked him across the back of his head with his chopper. Rich Loc stumbled forward, smashing his face into the back of the van and landing on his side. He bawled, while a knot formed on his forehead.

Chapter 11

"My nigga, you really ready to die over this pussy, huh?" Golden smirked, sticking his chopper between Aries's thighs and sticking his tongue out at her. She squeezed her eyes shut and tears jetted down her cheeks. Golden looked over his shoulder at Rich Loc, who was watching him with a scrunched face. His eyes were red-webbed and a large vein was at the center of his forehead. If it wasn't for him being at his mercy, Golden knew, without a doubt, he'd kill him. "A'ight, lover boy, play time's over. Either you gon' tell me what I wanna know, or I'ma blow her pretty lil head off," he threatened, pressing his AK into her temple.

Aries whimpered and squirmed, trying to get free of her bondage.

"Fuck you, fuck you," Rich Loc hollered at him.

"You've got until the count of five. One, two," Golden began counting, staring at Rich Loc's face.

Rich Loc looked from a weeping Aries to Golden, with his heart thudding. He had to make a decision, and he had to make it fast. Though he loved his money, he didn't love it nearly as much as he loved Aries.

"Four, fi—" Golden's countdown was cut short by Rich Loc interrupting.

"A'ight, a'ight, a'ight, I'll give you all I have, just don't kill my fiancée," Rich Loc told him. Golden smiled devilishly again and took the assault rifle from Aries's temple. Rich Loc and Aries sighed with relief.

"You've got a keepa, ma. This nigga really loves you," Golden told Aries. He sat down against the wall of the van on the opposite side of Aries. He couldn't help thinking of how much Rich Loc looked like a worm scooting over beside Aries. Rich Loc kissed her all over the side of her face and rubbed his cheek against hers. She snuggled up against him, whimpering, and he consoled her like any masculine man would his woman. "A'ight, Dunn, it's time for you to keep yo' end of the bargain."

"I got, like, two million that I keep at a self-storage unit," Rich Loc told him, like it hurt to do so.

Golden looked at him like he thought he was stupid. "My nigga, all that jewelry, fancy cars and loot you always flossin' around town. Am I really supposed to believe you only sitting on two mill? Come on, now."

"Cuz, that's all the money I've got in this world, word is bond." Rich Loc looked him dead in his eyes. "The rest of my money is tied up in my businesses and liquid assets. If you tryna get cho paws on that. Then, it's gonna take some time."

Golden nodded understandingly, while massaging his chin. "A'ight, Rich Loc, I'ma take yo' word for it, but what's up with them jewels?"

"I'ma keep it one hunnit witchu, bro. All that shit you seen a nigga rockin' ain't even real," Rich Loc confessed.

Golden's response was upping his chopper and aiming it at the kingpin's throat.

"I'm serious, loc. I don't think like your average dope-boy. Why buy the real thang, when everybody and their baby mama know you've got the bread to afford it? Whatever you see me in issa knock off. Besides my babies, my whips."

Golden used his chopper to point out the twinkling diamond engagement ring adorning Aries's finger. "What about that rock on yo' shorty's finger?"

"I said everythang I wear issa knock off," Rich Loc said. "Now, when it comes to my queen, she gets the best of everythang. Nothing fake, believe that." Golden kept his eyes on the engagement ring. "Lemme guess, you want that too?"

"Nah, regardless of what these niggaz say out here, there is honor among thieves." Golden finally looked up at him. "Now tell me where the money and the dope at?"

Rich Loc told Golden everything he wanted to know. He seemed to be disappointed that he only had ten birds stashed, which was in case of a drought. He managed to convince Golden that the rest of his drugs were circulating in the streets, and he wouldn't see a return on that investment for at least a week. Golden could have sat on Rich Loc and his lady until the bread came back around from the weight, but he figured that was being too greedy. And he firmly believed that being greedy was how most street niggas wound up getting killed or landing in jail. With that in mind, Golden made the decision he believed was in the best interest of him and his family.

"What time does this storage of yours close?" Golden asked.

"'Round eleven," Rich Loc replied.

"A'ight, check this out, we're gonna pick up another van and shoot up there." Golden told him before aiming his chopper at him. "But if I get the feelin' you tryna pull some fuck shit, I'm downin' you and Miss Thang over there. Ya dig?"

Rich Loc nodded and kissed Aries on top of her head

***

Golden borrowed another van from a cousin of his that lived out in Queens. At gunpoint, he forced Rich Loc to drive out to the storage facility, while Baby Girl, Shirvetta and Cowboy followed behind them in the other van. When they reached their destination, Baby Girl and them parked outside and waited for the transaction to be made. If shit didn't go right, they were to paint the inside of the van with Aries' brain. Golden was confident that Rich Loc wouldn't buck against them for fear of his lady marrying a bullet.

Rich Loc punched in the code on the keypad and the gate rolled back. He parked the van in the space closest to the tenement, and they hopped out. Golden looked around as he waited for Rich Loc to press in the code again at the keypad to the left of the automatic glass doors. He'd traded in his ski mask for a life-like mask that made him look like a brother in his late sixties. The automatic doors opened. Golden and Rich Loc walked inside, grabbed the pull carts and took the elevator to the 3rd floor. They opened the door of unit 3478 and pulled in the carts behind them.

The storage unit was spacious. It was full of boxes and other items, so it would look like the typical storage space. Golden stood behind Rich Loc, taking in his surroundings and trying to guess where the two million dollars was stashed. He got his answer when Rich Loc cracked open a cardboard box labeled "Books". He removed the books on the surface of the box and revealed stacks of blue face one hundred dollar bills.

"Here's one of the boxes, I'll grab the others." Rich Loc motioned Golden over to the cardboard box he'd just opened and went on to load the others on his pull cart. Golden picked up on the fact that all the cardboard boxes with labels written in red marker contained money. As they walked over to grab the last two boxes, Rich Loc spotted a cardboard box labeled "Pots and Pans". He recalled hiding a fully loaded .9mm Beretta inside that very box for situations like the one he was in now. Rich Loc figured if he could get his hands on that piece, he could take Golden hostage and exchange him for Aries.

As soon as Rich Loc got the idea in his head, Golden stepped in the path of the box he had his eyes on and looked him right in his face.

"I know what chu thinkin', *cuz*," Golden said, putting emphasis on the word *cuz*, imitating Rich Loc's vernacular. "Now, you've gotta strap somewhere hiding in one of these boxes. Somehow you've gotten it in your head to take me hostage and exchange me for your queen. That decision wouldn't be so wise. Your best bet is to continue what we agreed upon so you can get her back in one piece."

Rich Loc's eyebrows sloped and his nose wrinkled. "Cuz, how I know you're telling me the truth? You've gotta give me yo' word that chu gon' let us walk."

Golden sniffed and pulled on his nose. He took a step closer to Rich Loc, so they'd be eye to eye. "First of all, I don't gotta do shit. I've got the gun and I gotcho bitch. I'm the nigga with all the power, and you will do whatever the fuck I say, when I say it." He allowed what he said to soak into Rich Loc's brain, before he continued with what he had to say. "You've got my word though, son. You stick to the script, and you and yo' shorty can walk." He extended his hand to Rich Loc, who looked at it like he'd jacked off with it.

Taking a breath, Rich Loc went ahead and shook his hand. Unbeknownst to him, Golden had his fingers crossed behind his back.

"Now, come on, let's finish loading these boxes, so we can get that work outta the next storage." He patted Rich Loc on his back and walked over to one of the two boxes of money left.

***

Cowboy and Shirvetta were assigned to take the van with the two million dollars and the birds in it. They and Biggie were to unload the goods at the house and wait for Golden and Baby Girl, so they could divide everything equally. Baby Girl was tasked with driving Rich Loc and Aries to some place where they could be released. The entire ride to the location, Golden rode in the back of the van in silence. He kept his eyes on Rich Loc and Aries, who were snuggled up with each other, like puppies, trying their best to keep warm. Whenever Rich Loc would feel Golden's eyes on him, he glanced in his direction, and he'd quickly look away. Although he found this strange, he didn't think much of it. He reasoned that the honorable thief was enchanted by the beauty of his queen.

"A'ight, we're here," Baby Girl announced, putting the van in park, and leaving it idling. She'd exchanged her ski mask for a black bandana, which she'd tied around the lower half of her face.

Baby Girl grabbed her stick with the silencer and hopped out of the van. She was on her way to the opposite side of the transporting vehicle, when Golden tucked his piece in the small of his back.

"Remember our—gowp," Rich Loc was silenced by Golden stuffing a sock inside of his mouth and stretching a strip of duct tape over it. He pulled a black hood over his head, sentencing him to darkness.

Baby Girl opened the back doors of the van and a gust of wind greeted everyone. A few leaves managed to slip inside, but everyone ignored them.

"What's up with this nigga, bruh? You want me to leave 'em stankin' or what?" Baby Girl asked, while holding the back of Rich Loc's collar.

Golden looked at Aries, who had a saddened look on her face and tears in her eyes. She mouthed "please" and shook her head no. Keeping his eyes on her, Golden thought about how he should handle the delicate situation. He recalled the promise he had made, but if he kept it, he'd be putting his entire family in danger.

"Bruh?" Baby Girl called for Golden's attention. She was standing outside the van now, with Rich Loc in front of her and her stick pressed against his back.

Golden looked at his sister and then Aries again. She was still silently pleading with him as tears slid down her cheeks. Golden had always been a man of his word, so he decided to keep it. "Nah, I told homeboy I wasn't gon' drill 'em, as long as he kept his word. He did, so I'ma stand on what I said."

"Youz a lucky muthafucka, you know that? My bro has always been a man of principal—more so than the rest of his siblings," Baby Girl whispered in Rich Loc's ear.

"Sit tight, ma. I'm abouta tell you how we gon' play this," Golden told Aries as he picked up the other sock.

"Thank you. Thank you. Thank you," Aries mouthed to him. She placed a gentle kiss on his lips, relieved he kept his promise and didn't waste Rich Loc. Golden held her to him for a while, rubbing her back and kissing her on the forehead. He knew he was going against his gut instinct by not rocking Rich Loc to sleep. His decision could blow up in his face, but he was willing to risk it in the name of love.

Golden placed the sock inside of Aries's mouth and put a strip of duct tape over her lips. Cupping her face, he kissed her on the duct tape and then on her forehead. Picking up a black hood, he slipped it over her head and ushered her out the back of the van.

Outside of the van, in the woods, Baby Girl stood behind Rich Loc and Golden stood behind Aries. They both had their guns out by their side.

"A'ight, listen up," Golden began, speaking loud enough for everyone to hear. "On the count of three, I want you two to take off running, as fast as you can, until I tell you to stop, and not a minute sooner. Ya got that?" Rich Loc and Aries nodded. "Okay. One, two, three."

Rich Loc and Aries took off running, like someone had fired a round from a starter pistol. Golden and Baby Girl watched them for a while, before he nudged her and they climbed back inside of the van. Baby Girl started the van, backed up and drove away.

Chapter 12

"Ughh." Rich Loc collided with the ground.

"Ughh!" Aries collided with the ground beside him.

They lay beside each other, breathing heavily, exhausted from running. They never heard Golden or Baby Girl holler for them to stop, so they figured they'd already drove off. It took some time, but Rich Loc managed to work his head from out of the black hood. He looked around for something sharp to cut his restraints and his eyes landed on an 8-inch wood splinter. Rich Loc, with his back to the splinter, squatted down and picked it up. He sawed into the plastic zip-tie, until it broke in halves. After snatching off the duct tape, Rich Loc spat out the sock and removed the black hood from Aries's face. She winced when he peeled the duct tape from over her lips and yanked the sock out of her mouth. Grabbing her by the face, he kissed her like they hadn't seen each other in ten years, and then he hugged her like it had been twice as long since he'd touched her.

"Lemme getchu outta these thangs, shorty. Stand up." Rich Loc grabbed her under her arm and helped her to her feet. He held her by one of her wrists, while he sawed into the zip-tie, until it gave. Aries turned around, hugging and kissing on Rich Loc. She trembled as he held her in his arms. "You okay, shorty?" he asked, holding her chin up.

"I'll be fine. I'm just a lil cold," Aries replied, rubbing her hands up and down her arms.

Rich Loc removed his sports coat and draped it over her shoulders. He then grabbed her hand and fled through the woods. They looked like a couple of runaway slaves, with barking hounds and racist white men on their heels.

"Babe, where are we going?"

"Up to the road. Hopefully we'll come across someone traveling this way."

"How are you doing? I mean, you asked me but I didn't think to ask you."

"As long as my queen is straight, I'm gucci."

I don't know who these fools are that had the nerve to come at the Loc, but when I find out, it's up. Dead homies, Rich Loc thought, as they continued to make hurried footsteps past trees and whatever creatures lurked in the darkness.

***

Later that night...

Shirvetta, Cowboy, Biggie and Baby Girl were happy about the loot from the lick. Golden was too, but the interaction between Rich Loc and Aries was fucking with his mental, like a mothafucka. Although Aries was told to play her role with Rich Loc, like she'd been doing, it felt entirely too real for Golden's taste, especially when she begged him not to turn that nigga's lights out. Shorty cared just a little too much for him. She was behaving like dude was him, or some shit, and he wasn't feeling that at all.

Golden was having second thoughts about not murking Rich Loc now. Allowing him to live would probably come back to haunt him. The nigga was stupid paid and had connections that could get pretty much anyone touched. He was exactly the type of street nigga that you didn't want to play with. The blowback from getting at him was sure to kick up quite the shit-storm. He wasn't going to trip too much on the situation now, because what was done was done. Besides, it wasn't like Rich Loc knew him and his family's identities. And even if he did, he'd have to find them.

In the hood, word traveled fast about niggas being rats, bitches being hoes, dudes getting money and fools touching the streets after serving a bid. So, Golden was sure he'd catch wind when and if Rich Loc found out who was behind his kidnapping and robbery. The moment he got that information, he was going to be sure to come at him with everything he had. Not Aries or God himself would be able to save Loc from his wrath.

"Aye, nigga, fucks the matter witchu? You don't see all this bread in front of us?" Biggie asked, throwing a ten thousand dollar stack at his chest. He was still wearing Rich Loc's designer shades and his choker chain.

"Big bro, we're rich," Baby Girl said happily, hugging Golden around his neck and kissing him on his cheek. She had four stacks of blue faces in each of her hands.

"I can't front, son, this sure was a sweet, sweet lick you and ya girl put us up on," Shirvetta claimed with a smile, kissing Golden three times on the side of his face and throwing money up in the air. The cash came floating back down, like loose notebook paper.

"Son, look at this big ass nigga," Biggie smiled, pointing at Cowboy. He was laying on top of his cut of the money, staring up at the ceiling, smiling. The family doubled over laughing and slapping their knees. Cowboy couldn't hear shit they were talking about, though. He was wrapped up in his own thoughts, thinking about how high he'd be able to stay since he was sitting on some major chips now.

The twinkling diamonds of Rich Loc's chain caught Golden's eye. He looked at it with wrinkled brows and held it pinched between his finger and thumb. "Yo, whenever you fence this shit and that Lambo, make sure to do it far away from home. We don't want what we did tonight coming back to bite us in the ass."

"You ain't got nothing to worry about, big bro. I'm on it. I got everythang faded," Biggie assured Golden, shaking up and embracing him.

Golden massaged his chin as he gave the situation some thought. He cleared his throat and sat up in his chair. "I know a nigga we can unload this drop on."

"Who dat?" Shirvetta asked with wrinkled brows.

"Wood, ma," Golden replied. "You know Wood. He used to come to the house alla time. We went to junior high together."

"You mean, lil brown-skinned Wood, with the big nasty scar on the side of his head?"

"Yeah, that's bro," Golden said. "He doin' his thang over in Harlem now. My boy's kind of a big deal, nah mean?"

"Well, get 'em on the jack and see what he's talkin' about," Cowboy interjected, scratching his arm. He needed to see a street pharmacist to get his medication. He could feel the effects of his last dose wearing off.

Golden looked at Cowboy like he was covered in shit and flies were swarming around him. He was still hot about the stunt he pulled when they'd done the Chris Stacks job and how he'd backhanded Baby Girl. He wanted to get in his ass again about that, but this latest come up had him in good spirits, and he didn't want to dampen his mood.

"Relax, homeboy, I got this," Golden said, picking up his cellphone to make a few calls. He didn't have Wood's direct line but he knew a few people that could put him in touch with him.

"All you worried about is gettin' high, my G. You needa wean yo'self off that shit, before that old Mexican lady finds yo' ass like Jake found Skip in *Dead Presidents*." Biggie took the time to light up his cigarette.

"Ha, fuckin', ha," Cowboy said sarcastically, scratching under his chin now. "And for yo' info, lil nigga, old lady Mariana is Puerto Rican."

Biggie took the cigarette from his lips and blew out a cloud. "Same difference, bro. A spic is a spic."

"Aye, watch yo' mouth, my best friend is Rican," Baby Girl chimed in, as she entered the room.

"Which one of them chicken heads you run with is Puerto Rican?" Biggie inquired, taking another pull from his cigarette.

"Celeste," Baby Girl replied.

"What's up, sis? How you been?" Cowboy asked, grasping Baby Girl's arm. He was about to apologize for putting his hands on her, but shorty wasn't in the mood.

Baby Girl's face scrunched and she snatched her arm from him. "Don't chu ever, ever put cho fuckin' hand on me again, nigga, or I swear to God, I'll chop that muthafucka off." She wagged her finger in his face.

Cowboy jumped to his feet aggressively, like he was about to attack Baby Girl again. "Hold up, who the fuck you think you—" he was cut short by Biggie jumping up in his face.

"Whoa, big fella, we're not about to have another replay of what happened the other night," Biggie assured him, holding his gaze. "I'm not Golden. I'm not finna get all sweaty fightin' yo' big ass. Nah, see, that's not my game. I'm more of a shooter, if you know what I mean," he exclaimed, holding his pole down at his side. He'd drawn it the moment he saw his oldest brother grab his sister.

"Biggie, you gon' pull a strap out on me? I used to change yo' diapers. I showed you how to ride a bike, lil nigga. I got chu yo' first piece of ass," Cowboy spat heatedly. He was starting to feel like the outcast in the family, with everyone coming at him.

"Facts. But that's my lil sis, and I've taken an unspoken oath to love and protect her from everyone, brother included."

Cowboy's sawed off, double-barrel shotgun appeared in his hands, like a magic trick, and he shoved it into Biggie's gut. "You want me to go, son? I'll go, but when I leave, best believe I'm takin' yo' lil bitch-ass with me," he snarled, staring him in his eyes and clenching his jaws so hard, it felt like his teeth would break.

Cowboy and Biggie stared each other down for what seemed like a century. The entire time, Golden was in the background talking on the phone, while keeping an eye on them. Baby Girl stepped to the left of Cowboy and pressed her blue-steel .38 revolver to the side of his dome.

"You take that shotgun out of my brother's stomach, or so help me God, I'll—"

"Alright, now, that's enough. This has gone entirely too far," Shirvetta said, cutting Baby Girl short, and stepping between her sons. "Y'all cut this shit out now."

Golden's eyebrows slanted and his nose scrunched, seeing the scene unfold right in front of him. He finished writing down the number he was given and disconnected the call.

"Yooo, what the hell is up with you two niggaz, fam?" Golden asked, running across the room. "Say, bro, y'all needa relax. Y'all 'bouta blast each other in front of ma. Are y'all 51/50 or what?" He looked at the faces of his siblings. He couldn't believe there was a Mexican standoff between his brothers and sister. They used to all be so tight, coming up, but now they were fighting like cats and dogs, every other day.

"I'm gettin' tired of y'all playin' me like I'm some kinda bitch-ass nigga," Cowboy said, keeping his eyes on Biggie. "I'm the oldest of pop's pups, and I was the first to jump off the porch, bodying shit, I might add."

"Nigga, and? Fuck you tryna say?" Biggie spat, nostrils flaring.

"What I'm tryna say is I'll be damned. No, I'll be goddamned, if I allow my lil brothers and sister to treat me like I'm the runt outta the litter," Cowboy told Biggie. "Y'all better start payin' homage or—"

"Or, what, son? What?" Biggie asked, pointing his gun in his oldest brother's face, sideways.

"Y'all stop it, goddamn it. Y'all stop it right now," Shirvetta shouted, looking around at the faces of her children. She imagined them all as little boys and a girl again, while they stood there with their guns pinned on each other.

Golden looked at his siblings, without the slightest idea of what he should do to stop them from blowing each other away.

"Hmmph," Cowboy cracked a grin, lowering his sawed off. Baby Girl was next to lower her piece, and then Biggie.

Chapter 13

Smack. Smack. Smack.

Shirvetta went around the room, slapping all her kids, except for Golden. They all appeared to be shocked, especially Cowboy.

"What the fuck you hit me for, ma? That lil' nigga pulled his pole out on me first," a hot Cowboy shouted in his mother's face, while pointing at Biggie. She narrowed her eyes into slits to stop his spittle from getting in her face.

"True. But you're the oldest, so you know better," Shirvetta shouted back in his face.

"You're right. But all of these muthafuckaz are grown," Cowboy raged. He was so close to his mother their noses were touching and she could smell the stink on his breath.

"I said what I said. I'm your mother. You don't question me, *you're* my child" Shirvetta pointed her finger in his face. She was scolding him like a mother would her unruly child.

Cowboy grabbed his mother by her neck, squeezing her tightly and lifting her off her feet. She grabbed ahold of his hand and kicked her legs wildly. The veins in her forehead bulged and she turned red. Instantly, all of her children, including Golden, pointed their pistols at Cowboy. He was locked into such an intense stare down with their mother, it was as if they didn't exist to him.

"You've always had it out for me, 'cause I wasn't your biological son," Cowboy said, with teary-eyes and a locked jaw. "Growing up, I saw the difference you made between me and the ones that came outta you. They got special treatment, while I was made the red-headed stepchild. Pops was so pussy whipped he didn't see his oldest son was being neglected by the bitch he loved." Tears broke down his cheeks and his nostrils flared. He watched as his mother struggled in his clad-iron grip. "Tender dick ass nigga. That could never be me. You hear me? That could never be me."

"Cowboy, let mommy go before you kill her," Baby Girl shouted as tears slid down her cheeks. Still holding her pistol on him, she quickly wiped her eyes.

"Let her go," Biggie shouted, cocking the hammer of his gun back, preparing to shoot his sibling down.

"Cowboy, you're wildin' right now, bro. That's your mother," Golden told him. He'd drawn a bead on his brother's temple and could blow his head off, but he didn't want to do that. He wasn't sure if he could live the rest of his days with his brother's death on his conscience.

"Wrong, lil brother. This bitch is y'all's mother," Cowboy clapped back. "My Ma-duke abandoned me a long, long time ago."

"Cowboy, man, we needa sit down and hash all this shit out," Golden reasoned. "We needa get a therapist and discuss all this animosity between us, big bro. Like ma said, we're family. We shouldn't be at each other's throats like this." Golden became glassy-eyed, coming to the conclusion he may have to lie his oldest brother down.

Shirvetta had tears streaming down her cheeks and snot leaking out of her nostrils. Her movements were gradually becoming slower and slower.

"Cowboy, don't make me do this shit. I'm beggin' you, yo." Golden cocked the hammer back on his piece, to let Cowboy know he wasn't bluffing. "You've got 'til the count of five. I'ma count 'em out, one, two..."

Come on, bro, let her go. I don't wanna kill you, Golden thought. He stole a glance at Baby Girl and Biggie. They had tears sliding down their cheeks, as well. He knew their hearts and they were ready to cut their brother down just as he was.

Cowboy held his mother by her neck a little longer, before flinging her aside. She flew across the room and flipped over the pool table. She landed on her stomach, wincing and moaning in pain. Instantly, Cowboy's siblings rushed over to their mother, while he walked over to the pool table and picked up his hat. He walked around the pool table, where his brothers and sister were tending to his mother. Biggie and Baby Girl were mad dogging him, while Golden was comforting their mother.

"I'll be back here later to pick up my cut from tonight's lick," Cowboy told them, putting on his hat and adjusting it to his liking. He then gave them the once over and turned around to leave.

Angry, Biggie jumped to his feet with his pole, and moved to go after him. Golden grabbed him by his arm and he looked back at him. He could tell his baby brother was seething and wanted to get even with Cowboy for putting his hands on their mother, but now wasn't the time or place for it.

"Relax, lil bruh, you go after Cowboy now, and things are bound to get bloody," Golden assured him as he and Baby Girl pulled their mother to her feet.

Biggie snatched his arm from Golden and looked him in his eyes, saying, "That's what I'm lookin' for, Golden, blood."

"I feel you, son, I really do," Golden told him. "But let's not forget Cowboy is our big brother. He's family. We're all upset about the things he's done, but do you really wanna go spill his blood over it? You and I both know that once you take a man's life, there's no way to give it back. You needa seriously ask yo'self if you're ready to take the life of your own brother?" Golden looked from Biggie to Baby Girl. She lowered her head, which let him know, though she'd drawn down on Cowboy, she wasn't ready for the ill feelings that came with it. When he looked at Biggie, he got an entirely different reaction, though.

"If Cane can do his brother, I sure as hell can do mine." A scowling Biggie assured him and walked away.

Golden took a deep breath realizing it was going to be tough bringing his family back together. "Come on, Baby Girl, help me get ma over here on the couch."

With that said, they did just that and Golden went to go see a man about buying his bricks

***

Cowboy came up from the basement and walked towards the front door. He'd just placed his hand on the knob, when something came to his mind and stopped him in his tracks. He listened in on the basement door to see if anyone was coming, and then he went inside the kitchen. He grabbed a folded up Macy's shopping bag from underneath the sink and went through all the cabinets, until he found a bag of sugar. He smiled as he held the bag of sugar in his hand, testing the weight of it.

Cowboy walked out of the backdoor, locking it behind him. He entered the garage through the side door and flipped on the light switch. He grabbed one of the birds from where they'd stashed them for the time being. Keeping an eye on the garage door, he went on to swap the contents from the kilo with the bag of sugar. He resealed what was now the kilogram of sugar, licking the residue off his fingers during the process. Once he was done, he made sure the sugar bag containing the dope was secure, wrapped it up snugly inside the shopping bag and stashed it inside of his duster.

Cowboy walked out of the gate of the backyard, where the taxi he'd ordered earlier was waiting curbside for him. His cellular was glued to his ear, as he slid inside of the backseat and slammed the door behind him. As soon as his lady answered his call, they started chopping it up.

"What up, Cowgirl? What chu up to?" Cowboy asked, listening to what he was being told. "Well, I was thinkin' about us havin' a lil party tonight. I've already got the party favor." He smiled as he patted the bulging bag of dope inside of his duster's pocket.

***

Golden allowed Biggie to cool off before approaching him about riding with him to meet up with Wood. The youngest of Shirvetta's boys apologized for his initial reaction to his reasoning and admitted that he was right about his feelings towards Cowboy. The brothers dapped up and hugged it out. Then they strapped up and rolled out to holler at Wood. It had been a while since either of them had seen Wood, so they decided before they left they were going to handle him like anyone else they conducted business with.

"Ain't that Wood right there?" Biggie nodded toward a man standing beside a platinum-gray G-Wagon on chrome rims and tires.

Golden took a look before he replied. "Yeah, that's that nigga. I haven't seen homie in mad years."

"My guy done got a lot bigger, musta been hittin' the iron these last few years," Biggie said, making a mental note of how buff Wood had gotten since the last time he'd seen him. He was a scrawny nigga, back in the day, but he had some fight in him. Old Wood would lock ass with anyone. It didn't matter who the fuck they were.

Golden heard mad stories about Wood while he was locked up. Fools made it seem like he was the Antichrist or some shit, but he just took it as niggas putting extras on things, like they always did. What he knew for sure was that his childhood friend was a big stepper. They'd put in a lot of work together, so he definitely wasn't afraid to get his hands dirty. Wood was one hell of a shot, but his weapon of choice was a machete. He reasoned that they were more intimate than guns. A nigga had to be up close with a blade. He believed that if someone crushed their enemy with a knife, then their beef was on a personal level.

Golden backed his car into the parking space and killed its engine. He and Biggie hopped out and slammed their doors closed behind them. Golden smiled as he approached Wood, and he smiled back. Besides the muscle he'd packed on and the change in hairstyles, Wood looked the same as he did years ago. His head was shaved all the way around, while the rest of his hair was parted down the middle and braided into pigtails on either side. Like Golden, he had a body covered in tattoos.

Wood switched hands with the pickled pig feet he was eating and embraced Golden with a one arm hug. He shook up with Biggie and gave him a hug also.

"My young nigga, Biggie, son, I haven't seen you inna minute," Wood claimed, taking him in from head to toe. "I remember when you were yay high to a caterpillar, gettin' into all kinds a trouble, and tryna follow me and big bruh around the hood."

A grinning Biggie nodded, recalling his being a kid, following his big brother and his best friend around the neighborhood, like a stray dog they'd fed.

"I've heard a lot about chu out here, bro. I must say, the kid's impressed with your work." Wood nodded and shook up with him again. Biggie was known for jacking fools and walking shit down, throughout Brooklyn. He had a name outside of the Love Crime Family, just like his father, brothers, mother and sister. All of them combined made them a force to be reckoned with, so niggas got the hell out of the way when they saw them coming.

"Yo, son, I can say the same," Biggie said. "I mean, shit, who don't know about the boy Wood, from Bed-Stuy Do or Die? Every street nigga I've come across salutes yo' gangsta, nah mean?"

"Likewise, homeboy," Wood replied, sucking and eating his pig's foot. He then addressed Golden, who looked like he was disgusted by what he was eating. "How's the fam, son? We've got a lot of catchin' up to do."

Golden nodded, "Oh, we're gon' catch up, my nigga, no doubt. I just got out the bing a few days ago, so I'm tryna check some paper first. So, if you don't mind, I'd like to discuss business off the back, respectfully." He placed his hand to his chest. He knew humbleness and respect went a long way whenever two men were dealing with each other. The wrong choice of words could lead to a lot of tough talking and gun busting. Though Golden wasn't a stranger to danger, he'd like to avoid violence at all cost. He was just released from prison, and he wasn't in a rush to go back.

"Yeah, my G, we can do that." Wood ate some more of the pig's foot, wiped his mouth, balled the paper towel around what was left of it and tossed it aside. "You brought that sample of the product witchu, kid? I'm tryna see what chu workin' with."

"I got chu faded, my guy," Golden replied, tapping Biggie. Biggie pulled a small baggie of dope from out of his pocket and passed it to Wood. Holding it up, Wood scrunched his face and thumped the baggie.

Chapter 14

Later...

"Oh, yeah, this shit official. I can fuck with this," Wood said, after seeing the test results from the drugs. "Where did you get this shit from?"

Golden smirked, "Come on now, son. Don't get me to lying."

"How many birds you got, G? I'm tryna cop whatever you holdin'," Wood told him. "I mean everythang, ya feel me?"

"I got about fifteen of them thangs."

"You bullshittin'."

"Aye, I wouldn't bullshit a bullshitter."

Wood laughed and threw playful punches at him. "Fuck you, nigga. All jokes aside, what's the ticket on 'em?"

"You know the price tag on 'em is sixty in the streets," Golden reminded him, massaging his chin and thinking of a good price for his man. "Look, hit me with thirty a bird, how's that?"

"Nah," Wood shook his head no. "I'ma hit chu with at least forty a piece. You just came home, I'm tryna see you with a check. If I eat, I want my brother to eat, too."

"That's love, my nigga, Wood." Golden shook up with him.

"Mannn, youz a real ass nigga, Wood. I don't see how a nigga out here in these trenches can hate on you," Biggie told him, as he shook up with him, too.

"Believe me, Big, they'll find some kinda way to," Wood told him. "So, look, where are you tryna make this drop?" he asked Golden.

Golden scanned the area and looked back at Wood. "Shit, here is good. Let's make it happen at this spot."

"Nah, fam, I never meet up at the same location twice," Wood said. "Humans are creatures of habit, and habits lead to you gettin' all fucked up. I'm not tryna have that."

Golden nodded. He knew Wood was speaking some real shit. "A'ight fuck it. Let's say we link up at that lil spot over on…" he went on to tell him exactly where they should meet up for the drop. Wood was good with the location, so they agreed on a specific time.

***

Jade lay beside Cowboy on the mattress in the basement. Her eyes fluttered open. They searched the basement until they landed on a spider's web between the legs of the guardrails of the staircase. The eight legged creature crept towards a fly, who'd unfortunately managed to get caught in its web. Jade watched as the creepy crawly feasted on its meal, until Cowboy's snoring drew her attention. She sat up on the mattress, with her perky breasts exposed, looking over her shoulder at him. Cowboy was snoring with his mouth wide open and drool running out the corner of it. One hand was tucked inside of his boxer briefs, while the other was stretched above his head.

Jade scanned the basement for the sugar bag of heroin they'd indulged in last night. She located it underneath a couple of sleazy magazines strawn across the table on the other side of the room. A smile spread across her lips, as she planned to secure what was left of the bird and make a getaway. She looked from Cowboy to the dope to Cowboy to the dope, and then back again. He was still calling hogs, so she figured now was as good a time as any to make her move.

Jade put her bra and panties back on. Then she slipped on her clothes and shoes. Next, came her jacket and baseball cap. She eased off the mattress and snuck towards the table. She occasionally glanced at Cowboy to see if he was still sleeping. Gently, she removed the magazines off the sugar bag and picked it up. She peered inside of the bag, and when she saw the dope was still there, she smiled again. She'd rolled the bag back up and was about to stash it inside the pocket of her jacket, when she heard the hammer of a revolver cocking back. Her eyes bulged and her jaw dropped. She froze like someone had touched her in a game of Freeze Tag. Her eyes shot to their corners, where they saw Cowboy. His face was fixed with a scowl, and he had one of his pistols at her temple.

"I shoulda known yo' ho-ass would try to rob a nigga while he was catching some Z's," Cowboy told her. "I must say, I'm very, very disappointed in you, bitch. I thought we had somethin' beautiful between us."

"Boy, you must still be high 'cause you trippin' hard. I'm not tryna rob you," Jade replied, trying to run game. "I was just tryna, tryna—"

"Bitch, shut the fuck up. I'm a dope-fiend, not a dumbass," Cowboy reminded her. "Gimme my shit." He snatched the sugar bag from her and told her to turn around. Jade threw her hands up and slowly turned around to him. He could tell she was afraid but he didn't care. He reasoned she should have thought about that before she decided to steal from him.

"Cowboy, have mercy on me. I'm beggin' you. Please, please don't kill me," Jade pleaded, on the verge of tears, with trembling hands. She'd seen him drop plenty of bodies for one thing or another during their time together. Shit, some of them, she even went along with him to make sure they were properly buried, so she knew he didn't have a problem slumping her.

"Oh, I'm not gon' kill you, shorty," Cowboy assured her, lowering his stick at his side. "I am gon' kick yo' ass, though."

Cowboy hauled off and kicked Jade in her stomach. She painfully groaned and doubled over. He followed up by backhand punching her with the hand clutching his stick. The swift blow spun her around and she fell on all fours, breathing ragged. She spat blood and jabbed her loose tooth with her tongue. She spat it out and a string of blood hung from her bottom lip.

"Please, please, I've had enough—I can't, I can't take any—Ooof." Jade's eyes nearly popped out of their sockets when Cowboy kicked her in the stomach. She bawled on the floor, while he continued to work her over, stomping and kicking her viciously.

"I'll teach yo' no good, trifling-ass to steal from me, you funky, dope-head bitch," Cowboy shouted, kicking her in her mouth, and then stomping her head into the basement floor. Cowboy stared down at her as she lay unconscious, blood leaking from her grill. He turned around and walked away from her to get dressed.

***

Curtis and Joelle shot the breeze over a couple of beers on his front porch. Joelle did most of the listening, while Curtis did most of the talking. Most of his conversation revolved around his wife, who'd run off with another man, but Joelle didn't mind. His best bud needed an ear and he was happy to lend his. He'd experienced heartbreak before and it was absolute torture, so he felt Curtis's pain. To add insult to injury, a prisoner had handed him his ass right before his release, so he had two bitter pills to swallow. He was emotionally and physically hurt, and alcohol was just what the doctor had prescribed.

"You a'ight there, big dawg?" Joelle asked him, noticing the sadness in his eyes.

"Nah, Joe, I'm far from fucking a'ight," Curtis assured him, and snatched his state issued piece from its holster on his side. "I will be, though, as soon as I catch Golden and his bitch made ass brother slippin'. Nah mean?"

Joelle nodded his response and took another swig of his beer. Wiping his mouth, he watched Curtis aim his gun at a pyramid of empty beer bottles he'd made. He squeezed one eye shut and made a gun firing sound, pretending to shoot down the bottle at the very top. Holstering his piece, he took a swig of his beer and sat the bottle beside him.

Just then, a car screeched to a stop in front of his house. He and Joelle looked out into the street and found a '96 Chevrolet Caprice Classic. Curtis and Joelle pulled out their state issued pieces and made their way down the steps. They suddenly stopped when the passenger door swung open and someone was thrown out on the pavement. They couldn't see the driver's face as he reached over and slammed the passenger door shut. He then drove off, cranking up the volume on a throwback Jeezy song.

Curtis and Joelle exchanged frowns, wondering what the fuck was going on. The painful groans of the person lying in the street stole their attention. When they looked at them, they were trying to get back up on their feet and spitting blood. Their arms and legs wobbled as they tried to stand, and they crashed back to the ground. Joelle pulled his cellular out of his pocket, pressed the flashlight option and a light appeared. He shined the light on the person, who was thrown out in the street. He and Curtis were shocked when Jade looked up at them. She held her hand in front of her and narrowed her eyes, to combat the bright spotlight.

"Oh my God, my baby," Curtis said, voice cracking emotionally. He holstered his stick and ran over to Jade, kneeling down to her. He was having trouble helping her to stand. She grimaced with every move she made, being that she was aching all over.

"Help me, Joe. help me get her up and into the house." He threw her arm over his shoulders, snaked his arm around her waist and pulled her up on her sneakers.

Joelle put away his cellphone, holstered his stick and assisted his buddy with his wife. "Jesus, someone beat the hell outta her, Curt," Joelle mentioned, taking stock of her injuries.

Her face was swollen a blackish-blue, her eye was puffy and shut and she was bleeding at the mouth. On top of that, she was having trouble standing, like a newborn fawn.

"I know, I know, man," Curtis cried. Then, looking at Jade, he asked, "Who did this to you? Tell me who did this to you, sweetie, and I'll kill that muthafucka."

"It was—it was Cow—Cowboy," Jade replied weakly, as she was carried up the steps.

"I knew it. I fuckin' knew it," Curtis said with a drenched face and snotty nose. "I'ma body that big, black son of a bitch. I swear 'fore God, I'ma give his strung out ass a closed casket."

Curtis, Jade and Joelle went inside the house, and shut the door behind them.

***

Cowboy knocked on the front door of Shirvetta's crib. He watched his surroundings as he waited for someone to answer the door. The entire time he kept his hand on the gun in the pocket of his duster. With the lifestyle he and his family led, they had to grow eyes on the back of their heads to avoid a cemetery plot. Some may have called it paranoia, but he called it a survival instinct.

Cowboy looked back to the front door, as he heard its locks coming undone. When the door opened, a scowling

Biggie stood before him, with a gun at his side. He sucked on the end of a kush-filled blunt and blew a cloud of smoke in his face. Cowboy didn't bat an eye at the blatant disrespect. He was sure Biggie wanted some get-back for the way he'd handled his mother earlier. He was willing to play with the guns later, but now wasn't the time. He wanted his dough from that lick, and he didn't intend to leave without it.

"Look here, baby bruh, I didn't come here for no smoke. All I want is my cut from the job, and I'm gone," Cowboy told him with a dangerous glare.

Once again, Biggie took the opportunity to blow smoke in Cowboy's face before replying. "Son, I'ma give you yo' cut, but I want chu to know this. The only reason why I won't put something hot in yo' ass is 'cause I promised Golden I wouldn't. Otherwise, I'd pop you for how you did Maduke's, drag you up in here and have Baby Girl help me chop up yo' body, so I can dump it in the Hudson."

"I'm sure you would. Now fetch my fuckin' bag so I can go. It's cold as a bitch out here," Cowboy said, flipping the collar of his duster up to fight the cold.

Biggie left Cowboy on the doorstep, while he went to retrieve his money. He returned five minutes later, lugging a big ass duffle bag, which he dropped at Cowboy's feet. Cowboy kneeled down and unzipped the duffle bag. He peered inside at all the cash and looked up at Biggie.

"Do I needa ask?" Cowboy said, referring to if all his money was there.

"It's all there, nigga, plus yo' chicken from the bricks we sold to Wood," Biggie assured. He watched as Cowboy zipped up the duffle bag and picked it up.

Cowboy looked Biggie up and down, like he wasn't shit, before walking off.

"I swear 'fore God, the next time I see that fool, I'ma put 'em in the ground." Biggie's eyes lingered on Cowboy a while longer, before walking back into the house and slamming the door behind him.

Chapter 15

Days later...

Curtis pulled up outside a pool hall called Blue Streak and turned the engine off. He looked at Jade, who was wearing a New York Yankees baseball cap over her brows and five dollar Bodega shades over her eyes. She'd used makeup to try to hide the blackish-blue bruises on her cheek, but it did little to help.

"You sure you don't want me to handle this nigga for you? You know yo' man don't have no problem with rockin' this muthafucka to sleep," Curtis said, gripping her hand and caressing it.

"Yes. I'm sure," Jade confirmed with a weak smile. She looked up at the entrance of the establishment she planned to enter shortly. "Besides, this way is better. This way you don't have to get your hands dirty and risk going to prison. If we can get this man to have his people take care of things, we'll get our revenge and a bag. This will be a win, win for us."

Curtis nodded understandingly and kissed her hand. He pulled his piece from underneath the driver seat and chambered a copper round into its head before lying it in his lap.

"A'ight, lil mama, we're gonna do this your way," Curtis told her. "Go in there and holla at this fool and come back with that bag of money. If he tries to tug our dicks about the loot, then I'm callin' up my people and we're runnin' up in there bustin'."

"Understood," Jade replied, kissing him and hopping out of his whip.

Curtis watched closely as she pushed open the double doors of the pool hall and disappeared before his eyes.

***

"Yo, son, we've gotta problem." One of Wood's workers stepped inside the house, closing the door behind him.

"Big problem or lil problem? You know the rules," Wood replied, preparing a blunt. One of his rules, when it came to business, his underlings handled all the small problems, while he tended to all the big ones.

"Big problems, yo." The worker adjusted the beanie on his head.

Wood took the time to put fire to the tip of his blunt before responding, "Speak, or forever hold your peace, lil nigga." Wood sat back and outstretched his arm over the top of the couch.

The worker pulled out a packet with Wood's stamp on it and passed it to him. Wood smelled the contents of the packet and his nose scrunched. He dipped his pinky inside of the packet and tasted it. "This is sugar."

"Right. That entire last brick was sugar, son. Now we've got mad fiends at the spot bitchin' and complainin' about the product," the worker told him.

"I know you fuckin' lyin', Remo." Wood sat up on the couch, mashing his blunt out in the ashtray.

"I wish I was, big homie, but this real shit," Remo, the worker, told him. He watched as Wood picked his pole up from the coffee table and casually walked over to him. He swallowed his spit as his heart thudded crazily. He didn't know what Wood planned to do to him. He started to draw his stick but felt he'd be gunned down before he cleared it from his waistband.

Wood grabbed Remo by the front of his hoodie, forced him against the wall and pressed his stick underneath his chin. His face scrunched and he clenched his jaws. "My right hand to God, Remo, I swear if you and them niggaz down there are tryna finesse me, I'ma chop off y'all nut sacks and make coin purses out 'em."

Remo closed his eyes for a moment and took a breath. Wood had it bad about losing his temper and sonning his workers. He hated that about him, but looked the other way because he made good money with him. If it wasn't for that, and the fact he took him under his reign when he was roaming the streets like a stray dog, he would have been pumped Wood full of some hot shit.

"My nigga, you took me outta the streets and gave me a way to eat. I'ma be loyal to you 'til my last breath," Remo assured him. "Me nor any of the dudes under me had anything to do with this switch."

"You willin' to put cho life on that, Remo?" Wood looked him dead in his eyes.

Remo held Wood's gaze as he slowly removed the stick from underneath his chin and put it inside of his mouth. He bit down on the black plastic and steel before giving his answer. "My life and every last one of the lives of the niggaz under me."

Wood held Remo's gaze a while longer, before taking his stick out of his mouth. He patted him on his cheek gently, and then gave him a one arm hug. He kissed him on his temple and held him at arm's length.

"My bad, Remo, I shouldn't have come at chu like that," Wood told him. "It's just that this is a dangerous game we're playin' and I never know who I can trust. This will never happen again. I hope you can find it in yo' heart to forgive yo' big homie."

Remo was silent for a moment before nodding yes. He shook up with Wood and gave him a thug hug. "It's all good, my G. I vouch for my people, so if it isn't them, then who do you have in mind? If anybody?"

Wood turned away from Remo, exhaling and running his hand down his face. He then turned back around to him. "If it wasn't one of ours, then it was the nigga I got it from. The cold part about it is I've known this nigga for as long as I can remember, B. We're not related but he's as good as blood in my eyes. Nah mean?"

Remo nodded. He had a couple of homies he considered family and he'd hate to think they'd play him like Wood's man had obviously played him.

"Look, Wood, man, if you're thinking about lettin' homeboy slide then—"

"Fuck, no," Wood snapped. "I'm not lettin' shit slide, bitch-nigga didn't consider our history before he did what he did. Now did he?"

Remo shook his head, no.

"Gather a couple of shooters. It's time we show this nigga he fucked with the wrong one."

***

Golden threw his head back, yawning and stretching. He looked at the clock and realized he'd slept most of the day. He and Biggie had one wild ass night at Off the Wall, drinking, smoking, and tricking off with half-naked women. Though that night's fling was a blur to Golden, Biggie had captured it on his cellphone, so they could relive it. Golden caught an Uber home, to find Aries absent. She'd left a letter notifying him that she'd be spending the night with Rich Loc. At that moment Golden was hot, but then he reminded himself that his shorty had to continue to play her role, for the time being. When the perfect time presented itself, he'd lower the hammer and squash Rich Loc's bitch ass, once and for all.

Golden picked up his cellphone from the coffee table, where it was lying beside his gun. When he looked at the display of his cell, he had fifteen missed calls, and eight of them were from Aries.

Lemme see what's the deal with shorty. I ain't spoke to my boo all day, Golden thought. He was about to press the redial option on his cellular, when the living room's windows imploded, as Molotov cocktails were hurled through them. The burning glass bottles shattered on the carpet and flames scattered in every direction. The fire roared angrily as it worked its way throughout the house.

Automatic gunfire came through the walls and broken windows. Debris and clouds of smoke filled the living room. So many bullets were being pumped into the house it felt like a 7.0 earthquake had hit the city. Golden squinted his eyes as he crawled towards the coffee table and grabbed his gun off of it. He waited until the gunfire ceased and fled to the kitchen. He blasted off the backdoor's lock, kicked the door open, and escaped into the night's cool air.

***

The five masked gunmen on Golden's front lawn lowered their AK-47's with the one-hundred round drums. The collective stared up at the burning house, admiring their handiwork, while police car sirens wailed in the distance. Wood, who stood at the forefront of the masked shooters, smiled demonically behind his mask. Excitement appeared to dance in his eyes, watching the raging fire. It was like the anarchy he had created gave him a 12-inch hard-on.

"Yes, yes, yes, now this, this is beautiful. Abso-fuckin'-lutely beautiful," Wood claimed, laughing like a fucking maniac. He pointed his assault rifle above his head and squeezed its trigger. A burst of fire spat from its barrel and empty shell-casings flew from it. Wood lowered his assault rifle and took one last look at the raging fire.

Urrrrrk!

A black Cadillac Escalade halted in the middle of the street. One of the masked shooters hung out of the back window, calling for Wood and motioning him over to the SUV.

"Come on, man, Jake comin'," The masked gunman shouted.

Wood took his AK-47 into both hands and retreated towards the Cadillac Escalade. He hopped into the front passenger seat and the truck sped away before he could close the door completely.

A moment later, Golden ran from the side of the house, coughing and fanning the smoke from the fire. He ran out into the street just in time to see the Escalade truck hang a right at the end of the block. Turning around, he looked up at his burning house. Little by little, the residents of the neighboring houses began emerging from their homes, to see what was going on.

Niggaz done cocktailed my shit and sprayed it, Golden thought as he tucked his stick in his waistband. He turned on the faucet and used the water hose to combat the fire. *There's only one muthafucka responsible for this, and when I catch up with 'em, I swear 'fore God, he's gon' wish they kept my ass locked up.*

Golden's face twisted into a mask of hatred as he clenched the hose. A fire truck and a couple of police cars pulled up behind him.

Chapter 16

Jade pushed open the doors of Blue Streak and was greeted by Al Green's *Love and Happiness*, the scent of cheap cigars, nicotine and the conversations of patrons. If they weren't conversing, they were drinking, dancing or playing a game of pool. Jade ran her eyes over the scenery before heading over to the bar. The bartender had just sat someone's alcoholic beverage in front of them when she called for his attention. He made his way down to her end of the bar, as he wiped it down. He asked her what he could get for her and she motioned him to lean toward her.

"My name's Jade. Rich Loc's expecting me," Jade told him, pulling out a twenty dollar bill. She straightened the wrinkles in it, held it up for him to see and then passed it to him. "Just a lil somethin' for your troubles."

"I'll be right back," the bartender replied, pocketing the bill and tossing the towel over his shoulder. He turned his back to her as he picked up the black telephone and dialed up whomever. He stared at Jade through the mirror behind the bar while he talked, and she looked over the surroundings, pretending she didn't know he was watching her.

Two minutes later, the bartender was hanging up the telephone and walking back up to Jade. He tapped her shoulder for her attention and she spun around on the stool. She lifted her eyebrows at him like, *What's up?*

"You can go ahead and make your way around the corner there. You walk to the end of the hallway, make a left and you'll see a big old blue door with a black sign that reads *owner*, to your right. You can't miss it."

Jade nodded and thanked him, before following his directions. She knocked on the door and scanned the corridor, as she waited for someone to answer. She got the strangest feeling someone was watching her from the peephole in the door but she quickly shook it off. Jade listened to what sounded like one thousand locks coming undone before the door was pulled open. She was expecting to see a man, but instead, she came face to face with one sexy ass woman. Her hair was braided into a unique design of cornrows with stylish baby hairs along her hairline. A royal blue bandana was tied around her head, and she was wearing a matching short sleeve Dickie suit. The gold tennis necklace hanging around her neck had a nametag, *Rich Loc's,* so niggas and bitches would know she was his property. The end of her Dickie shirt was tied up to display the diamond stud piercing in her navel, as well as the beautiful red roses inked around her lower region.

The woman who'd unlocked the door was sucking on a blueberry Tootsie Roll pop and holding onto the blue leash of a German shepherd. The gold, black and white hound had a royal blue bandana tied around its neck. Jade took a step back when the beast started growling at her. She swallowed the lump of fear in her throat and slipped her hand inside her back pocket. She had a switchblade she wasn't afraid of using, if the dog was feeling froggy.

"I take it you're Jade, am I right?" the woman asked.

Jade and the dog were locked in an intense glare when the question was posed, but she nodded, yes.

"Cool. Come on in." She motioned her inside with the hand that held her sucker.

Jade took one step forward. The German shepherd stood his ground and started barking at her. Jade's heart nearly leaped out of her chest. Swiftly, she drew her knife and triggered its 3.4 inch blade.

"Gangsta, cut that shit out, nigga." The German shepherd instantly shut its mouth. The woman looked at Jade and then her switchblade. "You good, sis, he doesn't bite."

Jade twisted her lips as she cocked her head aside. She gave her that *Bitch, be serious* look. "A'ight, look, lemme put 'em inside the other room so we can talk business."

Once the woman put the dog inside the other room, she ushered Jade in and locked the door behind her. Jade stood at the center of the office, taking in the decor of the office space. There was a 60-inch flat screen on all four walls, blue leather furniture, a blue lighted wall-to-wall aquarium with gray, cold-stunned, carnivorous sea turtles, and a mural of Rich Loc as a blue bandana rocking war chief. Jade was astonished by the mural. It was very lifelike. She was about to touch it, when the woman calling for her attention startled her.

When she turned around, she found the woman sitting behind the desk. Her blue Chuck Taylors were propped up on the desk, and she'd traded in her Tootsie Roll pop for a cigar. She motioned Jade over to take a seat. Holding the cigar in her mouth, she twisted it back and forth, while roasting it with the flame of a zippo lighter.

The woman blew out a cloud of smoke before addressing Jade. "Rich Loc had some business he had to attend to so he left me here to conduct this deal on his behalf. I hope you don't mind."

"I really don't care who I talk to, as long as I get the money for the info I give you."

The woman nodded understandingly. "I hear you, 'money talks and bullshit walks'."

"Exactly."

"Okay. Here's the deal," the woman began. "You tell me who this nigga is that stole from Rich Loc, and I'll give you half of the hunnit bandz. You get the other half once the information is confirmed. Cool?"

"Nah. How do I know that you won't just pay me half, and run away with what I give you, without paying me the other half?"

The woman took another pull from her cigar and pressed the button underneath the edge of her desk. It flashed blue on and off, then the office door swung open. Jade looked over her shoulder as what looked like a dozen buff, tattooed gangsters poured into the office. They were all wearing a blue bandanas, either around their heads or somewhere on their bodies. The guns in their waistbands gave Jade cause for concern, but she wasn't about to let them see her sweat.

"Lil mama, let me assure you, if I wanted that info you're harboring in that brain of yours, then I'd gladly have my goons here beat it outta you." The woman mad dogged her.

"Well, they'd have to beat me 'til I was dead 'cause I'm not coming up off shit. Besides, I don't think they could do worse than what ol' boy did," Jade said, removing her baseball cap and then her shades. She shook her hair free and combed her fingers through it. The woman was taken aback by the damage done to her. She stubbed out her cigar in the ashtray on the desktop, and sat back in her executive office chair.

"I take it homeboy that gave you those beauty marks is the same one that stole Rich Loc's shit."

Jade nodded, as she slipped the shades back on, and then her baseball cap.

The woman massaged her chin, as she gave the ordeal some thought. She laid her eyes back on Jade, before continuing what she had to say. "A'ight, Jade, I'ma give you the full amount for the name and whereabouts of this lil thieving ass nigga."

"Good. Then we have ourselves a deal," Jade said, extending her hand over the desk. The woman stared at it for a moment before shaking it.

The woman that Jade had come to see was leaning over her desk, running stacks of money through the counter. Jade and the gangsters lingered around, listening to the sound of the money shuffling through the counter. Once this last stack was accounted for, the woman tangled a beige rubber band around it and tossed it inside of the knapsack on the floor beside her leg. She zipped the knapsack up, and slung it over to Jade.

"It's all there, sis, one hunnit big ones," the woman told her. She then picked up the sheet of paper she'd jotted the info on that Jade had given her.

Jade stood up smiling, slipping the strap of the knapsack over her shoulder and outstretching her hand to the woman. "It was nice doing business witchu, uh, you didn't gimme your name."

The woman stood up and shook her hand. "'Round here, they call me G-Mama, Gangsta Momma, or Gabby."

Jade nodded, slipped the other strap of the knapsack over her shoulder and made her way towards the door. The gangsters parted like the red sea, and gave her a clear path to the office's exit.

***

Cowboy sat back on the La-Z-Boy chair with a tourniquet tied around his arm and a syringe of dope. Licking his ashy lips, he went to enter what he called the Gates of Heaven, when his cellphone rang. He started to ignore whomever it was interrupting his moment, but something was nagging him to see who it was.

Cowboy sat the syringe aside and picked up his cellphone. Pop's was on the display. Staring at the screen, he tried deciding whether he should answer the call or call him back later. Once the ringing stopped and started back up again, he figured it had to be something serious, so he answered it.

"What's up, old man?" Cowboy picked up the call.

"Junior, what the hell is going on out there?" Heavy began. "Ya mom's tells me you threw hands with Golden, put hands on Baby Girl, and tossed her ass like a rag doll. You lost it, kid. I don't know if it's the dope or what, but you need to see about getting yo'self some serious fuckin' help. I can't have you harmin' anyone in this fam—"

"But muthafuckaz in this family can harm me, though, right?" Cowboy snapped, with tears in his eyes and nostrils flared. "I bet cho punk-ass wife didn't say a goddamn thang about her pups pulling out straps on me, and putting 'em to my muthafucking head, did she?"

"Look, son, I understand you're upset, but watch yo' mouth when you mention my wife and yo' moth—"

"Fuck that bitch."

"Excuse me?"

Cowboy turned around in time to see silhouettes moving across the basement window. His brows furrowed, wondering what the fuck was up. He quickly grabbed his revolvers. He tucked one in his waistband and held the other at his side.

"You heard me, muthafucka. Fuck that bitch. She killed my muthafuckin' momma and you helped her dispose of her body."

"Junior, what are you talkin' about? Yo' momma abandoned us, left you and me."

"Youz a fuckin' liar, bruh. I saw Shirvetta kill my momma with my own eyes. I saw you in the bathroom with her cuttin' up her body," Cowboy's voice cracked with hurt and tears broke down his cheeks. He snorted and spat on the floor. "You and that trifling skeeza tried to convince me I was having nightmares and that none of that shit I witnessed was real. Had a young nigga thankin' he was crazy and shit. I turned to dope to cope with this shit that's been haunting me, yo. The only thang that made me feel better was getting high, getting pussy, and juxin' these weak-ass niggaz out here."

Heavy was silent. He didn't know what to say. This entire time, he thought him and Shirvetta had pulled the wool over Cowboy's eyes.

Chapter 17

"Yo' scandalous-ass gon' come to my house and threaten me behind some dick that wasn't yours in the first fuckin' place? How dare you," Chick grunted and clenched her jaws, veins bulging on her forehead.

"Ain't my fault you don't know how to keep a fuckin' man," Shirvetta grunted with a balled up face. She was slowly losing the battle for control of the gun.

The women's' shadows danced across the walls, as they fought over the gun. They knocked over furniture and vases, and a portrait fell off the wall, before the pistol fired again. Instantly, the racket they were causing stopped. Chick, looking shocked, and staggered backwards, holding her stomach. She looked at her hand and it was bloody.

A shocked look was on Shirvetta's face. She looked at the smoking gun in her hands and then at the hole she'd put in Chick's belly. Looking at Shirvetta made Chick angry all over again. Her face scrunched and she charged at her screaming. Shirvetta lifted her pistol again, aimed, and fired twice. A second bullet struck Chick high in the chest, while a third melted into her face. She fell back on the couch, wide-eyed, with her mouth open. She was dead.

Shirvetta put her warm gun inside of her purse, pulled a latex glove over her hand and took out a hunting knife. She closed Chick's hand around the knife's hilt to get her prints on it, and then tossed it beside her on the couch. She peeled off the glove and tossed it inside of the kitchen's trash can. Her cellphone vibrated. She answered it.

"Hey, mommy's lil' man, what're you doing up? Grandma's sleep? So you're up alone. Well, do mommy a favor and try to get some rest. I'll be there later to pick you up. Aww, mommy loves you too, Golden. Bye, bye." Shirvetta disconnected the call. Closing her eyes, she took a deep breath and prepared to put on an Oscar worthy performance.

"Heavy, you've gotta come quick. No, no. I'm at your place. It's about Chick. I can't say over the phone. Just hurry." She disconnected the call and dropped her cellular back inside of her purse. Her brows wrinkled when she got the eerie feeling someone was watching her. She whipped around in hopes of catching someone behind her, but there wasn't anyone there.

Shit, I forgot about Junior, Shirvetta thought, before creeping down the hallway. She opened Cowboy's bedroom door and snuck a peek inside. When she found him asleep, she sighed with relief and closed the door back. A car's door slamming outside alerted her to Heavy's arrival. She ran back into of the living room in time to see him locking the door behind him and turning back around. His eyes widened and his mouth hung open, when he saw Chick lying dead on the couch. He walked toward her, dropping his thermos and his lunch box.

"Oh, no, no, no, no, not my baby." Heavy's eyes watered. He plopped down on the couch beside Chick and pulled her into his arms. Tears streamed down his face, as he caressed her cheek. He looked up at the ceiling, wearing an ugly expression across his face. "Look, man, I know I've done a whole lotta bad, but I've changed my ways. I've been doin' good. So, I'ma need you to leave her here. You hear me? Oh, Christ, you can't do this, man. This is my baby boy's mother." Heavy broke down sobbing, kissing Chick's forehead and begging her to stay with him.

Shirvetta had never seen Heavy show such emotion before. Seeing him so vulnerable made her sad and jealous, at the same time. She knew she couldn't allow what she was feeling on the inside to register on the outside because her plan would backfire. Shirvetta mustered up a fresh batch of tears and went to approach Heavy, reaching out to him. She jumped back when he suddenly hopped up from the couch and brushed past her. He nearly knocked her over, but she could tell by the look on his face, he didn't give a fuck.

"Heavy, where are you going?" Shirvetta called after him.

Before she knew it, he had returned to the living room with a nickel-plated, pump action shotgun. Tears poured from his pink eyes non-stop, as he racked the shotty and upped it on her. Shirvetta was visibly shaken now and wanted to try for her gun. The only thing stopping her was fear of being blown away before she could draw it from her waistband.

"Shirvetta," Heavy began, voice cracking emotionally. He took the time to swallow the lump of hurt in his throat and gather himself. "I need you to start talkin' fast, and be forewarned that whatever you say better make a whole lotta goddamn sense, 'cause if not, you gon' find yo'self lying right beside my baby. Do you understand?"

Shirvetta nodded her head slowly and wiped a lone tear that escaped down her cheek.

"Good. You're on the clock. You've got twenty-seconds, starting now."

"I came over here to hash things out with Chick. I thought we could make up and raise these babies together, as a family," Shirvetta told him. "She wasn't tryna hear that, though. She started mouthing off about how she wasn't sharing her man, or her son, with me, or any other bitch. I told her that you weren't gon' have that 'cause you always said you wanted to raise the boys together. She was like you're…you're right…" She broke down sobbing, but pulled herself back together to finish telling her story. "The only way I'm gonna, I'm gonna be able to keep my family to myself is if your ass is gone. That's when she drew that big ass knife outta nowhere, we wrestled over it..."

"Seven seconds," Heavy told her, lying his finger on the trigger.

"She was about to cut me, but then I remembered I brought the gun with me, the one you left at the house when you moved out. I wanted to give back to you," Shirvetta said. "Heavy, I swear on Golden and the twins that's growing inside of me, she had that knife to my throat with every intention of slittin' me open. I kicked her off me and she fell back on the couch. She went to rush me and I, and I, and I—" Shirvetta's head dropped and her shoulders slumped. Her head bobbed as she cried long and hard.

Heavy lowered his shotgun at his side. He took a deep breath and pulled her into him. He sniffed snot back up his nose, as he comforted her. Although he was satisfied with the story she gave him, it didn't stop his heart from aching. Losing Chick was like losing a part of himself. Shorty was the only woman he'd ever loved, besides his grandmother. He was confident this one was going to hurt for years to come.

"Wait a minute, what about Junior? Did he witness any of this?" Heavy asked, with worry in his eyes.

Shirvetta shook her head, no. "He was asleep the entire time."

"Good. That's good." He ran his hand down his face.

"Baby, what are we gonna do?"

Heavy looked at Chick's lifeless body and then back at Shirvetta. "Well, from what chu told me, you were defending yo'self. You can beat this all day long. The only problem that'll arise is that burner of mine and that illegal ass silencer that's on it. You'd be lookin' at a felony, punishable by up to three years in county, maybe even the pen, but that's only if it's your first offense. We both know that this ride won't be your first, you got priors."

"I know. That's exactly why I can't afford to deal with the law. You know how they do our people."

Heavy sat down on the arm of the couch, laying his shotgun across his lap. "Indeed. So what do you suggest?"

Heavy looked into Shirvetta's eyes and he knew off top what she wanted him to do. He shook his head. He couldn't see himself doing that to someone he loved, especially not Chick.

"I know, I know. It seems fucked up but it's the only way I can see my way outta this. Remember, baby, I've got priors. We get One Time involved, I wind up facin' some cracka ass judge, he's definitely gon' throw the book at me," Shirvetta told him, cupping his face and giving him the saddest eyes. "Then instead of being without one of your kids' mothers, you'll be without both. This way, at least I'd be around for our children. I'll raise Junior like I pushed 'em outta me, just like the rest of my babies. He'll never know the difference." She placed Heavy's hand on her belly.

Heavy's forehead wrinkled when he felt a kick. He looked to his right at something that had caught his eye. It was a portrait of him, Chick and Junior. Then he looked at another portrait that had him, Cowboy and Golden. He knew then he couldn't afford for his children to lose both mothers.

"Okay. I'll do what needs to be done." Heavy nodded with saddened eyes.

Shirvetta kissed him and threw her arms around his neck.

"I need you to look out in the garage and get my old tool bag. You know the one. Hurry up. There's no time to waste. I don't want Junior waking up and seeing something he shouldn't have."

"Alright. I'll be right back." She kissed him on his forehead, caressed his cheek and walked away to carry out his request.

Heavy glanced back at Chick, fighting back tears. "Forgive me for what I am about to do, baby, but it must be done for a better good," his voice cracked under his raw emotions. He felt like he was about to break down again, but he held strong.

Heavy hoisted Chick over his shoulder and carried her into the bathroom. He stripped her naked and laid her down inside of the tub. He then covered the floor in garbage bags to catch any blood splatter.

Shirvetta brought his leather 'tool bag' into the bathroom and unzipped it. They got dressed in a shower-cap, surgical mask, insulated suit, latex gloves, and shoe coverings. They drained Chick's body of its blood, chopped it up, and began storing the severed parts inside of separate garbage bags.

Unbeknownst to them, Cowboy had been watching them through the crack of the bathroom door. His innocent young eyes widened in shock from the atrocity he had witnessed. He wiped away his tears and walked away from the door.

Heavy looked at the bathroom door but there wasn't anyone there. He could have sworn he felt someone's presence over his shoulder.

"What is it, baby?" Shirvetta asked, placing a severed leg inside one of the garbage bags. She could tell something was troubling him by the expression on his face.

Heavy pulled the surgical mask down from his nose and mouth. "I think my son was at the door."

"What? I didn't see anyone, and I'm facing the door." Shirvetta frowned, looking from him to the door and then back again.

Heavy removed everything, as fast as he could, and headed out of the bathroom. Shirvetta called him back and he turned around. "Where you going?"

"To check on baby boy, whadda you think?" Heavy said, before disappearing into the hallway. He twisted the doorknob of Cowboy's bedroom door and gently pushed it open. He watched Cowboy as he slept, looking for any signs of him having been out of bed. He didn't see any.

Heavy pulled the covers up on Cowboy and kissed him on his temple. He shut the door behind him and moved to walk away, when he thought he heard whimpering. Frowning, he held his ear to the bedroom door and listened for the sound again. When he didn't hear anything, he walked back to the bathroom, where he continued with the dismemberment of his baby's mama's body.

Heavy was ignorant to Cowboy having witnessed his participation in the butchering of his mother. The whimpering he'd heard after leaving Cowboy's bedroom had definitely come from him. What he'd seen done to his mother fucked with his mind, and he cried until he fell asleep.

Cowboy was heartbroken upon the revelation that his mother didn't love him, and his father had abandoned him. Heavy had convinced the boy that what he'd seen him doing to his mother's corpse was a nightmare. The poor child was hurt and confused, but he chose to believe his father.

Cowboy began acting out at school and running with a group of young, ruffians who did whatever they had to for a quick buck. His causing chaos made him feel better, to a degree, but it wasn't until he discovered dope that he found a temporary relief to his pain.

Chapter 18

Cowboy strapped on a bulletproof vest and shattered the light bulbs so niggas couldn't see him, once they rushed the basement. "You ain't got shit to say now, huh, old nigga? You were just a Chatty Patty a minute ago, now yo' ass quiet and shit. You crossed yo' eldest son and stabbed his mother in the back. The kid ain't got no love fa nan one of you bitchez no more. Fuck this family and fuck you. From now on, it's up." Cowboy disconnected the call and pocketed his cellphone.

***

Mariana crooned softly as she cooked what was her tenant's favorite Puerto Rican dish. At sixty-four-years-old, she stood five-foot-two and weighed a total of two-hundred-and-thirty-two pounds. A pair of eyeglasses decorated her face. She wore her salt & pepper hair combed to the back and it hung just past her waist.

"Hey, there, Senor Fluffy. How would you like to taste some of mama's salsa?" Mariana smiled down at her cat, who was sniffing around the stove. She dipped her wooden spoon into her homemade salsa and let Mr. Fluffy lick some of it. She took a few licks of the spoon and put it back in the small pot of salsa. She added a little more seasoning to it and went back to singing and stirring the contents of the pot.

Mariana was so caught up in her routine, she neglected her surroundings. She sang over the sound of the backdoor's lock being picked and three masked men creeping into the kitchen right under her nose. They were holding Glocks with auto sears, which made the semi-automatic pistols fire like fully automatic firearms. The leader of the three man hit-squad turned to the other two hitters with his finger to his lips. They nodded and their leader stood upright. Holding his stick up at his shoulder, he placed his back against the wall. He was about to make his next move when that puss' ass cat caught his eye. Mr. Fluffy's ears laid back as he hissed and displayed his fangs.

"Fuck," the leader said under his breath. He knew that goddamn cat was going to ruin their element of surprise.

Growling, the hostile feline leaped from the counter with every intention of clawing out his eyes. The leader pointed his stick at Mr. Fluffy and pulled its trigger. In midair, the cat exploded into globs of blood, meat and fur.

The burst of gunfire startled Mariana. She staggered back with her hand over her long titties. She got the surprise of a lifetime, when she saw what was left of Mr. Fluffy. Tears burst from her eyes and she was overcome with grief. When she saw the reflection of the hitters in the toaster, she gasped and retreated to the walk-in pantry. The hitters invaded the kitchen, looking around for her, but she wasn't anywhere to be found. They scowled behind their masks, when Mariana seemingly appeared out of thin air with a double barrel shotgun. It was huge. In fact, it was so huge it didn't look like she was capable of firing it without flying backwards.

"You pinche putos fucked up breakin' into mi casa," Mariana told them with pink, glassy eyes and snot peeking out of her nose. Mr. Fluffy's death was equivalent to that of a family member, so she felt the loss at the very depths of her soul.

"Look here, old lady, put that shotgun away 'cause you and I both know you aren't prepared to—" the hitter's words died in his throat, as the barrel of the shotgun exploded. The hitter flew backwards into the kitchen cupboards, dropping his Glock and colliding with the floor.

Mariana turned the lethal end of her shotgun on the next hitter, but before her finger could curl around the trigger, he and his comrade unloaded on her. Dropping the shotgun, Mariana staggered back fast, knocking over the pot of salsa and crashing to the floor.

The hitter who'd gotten blasted, lay on the floor wincing. The other two hitters tended to him, trying to see how badly he'd been injured.

"Yo, son, you good?" one of the hitters asked.

"I'll be a'ight, yo. Shit hurts like a muthafucka, but none of the bucks made it through," the hitter replied between winces. He extended his gloved hand and his comrade pulled him up.

They looked to the hitter that had led the charge. He signaled for them to be quiet, as he snuck out of the kitchen and to the basement door. He pressed his ear against the basement door and listened in, while his comrades stood behind him. He twisted the knob gently and found it locked from the other side. He whispered to his comrades what he had in mind, before stepping back and kicking the door wide open. The basement was pitch black and he couldn't see jack shit. He started to creep down the staircase, but something told him it was best he sent one of the other guys.

"Daboo, you take the lead. Jynx and I will back you," Parelli, the lead hitter, whispered to the hitter who'd tended to the one who'd gotten blasted by the old Puerto Rican lady.

"Back me up? Son, you expect me to go waltzin' my ass down in there, without knowing what's waiting for me?" Daboo whispered back, looking at Parelli like he was bat shit crazy.

"Look, nigga, I'm runnin' this show, and I say you take yo' bitch-ass down there first," Parelli spoke through clenched jaws, smacking him across the back of his head and kicking him in his ass. He stumbled forward and nearly fell down the staircase.

Parelli and Jynx stood behind Daboo, as he prepared to make his way down into the basement. Taking a deep breath, he crossed himself in the sign of the Holy crucifix and slowly crept down the staircase. He tried to be as quiet as he could, but the squeaking of the eighth step gave his location away.

Blam, blam, blam, blam.

Bullets broke up the wooden steps, striking Daboo in his leg, knee, thigh and dick. Daboo hollered in excruciation, dropping his piece and tumbling down the staircase fast.

"Ahhhh, fuck. My dick, my balls. Arrrrh," Daboo hollered from where he lay on the basement floor. He continued to holler, until a single gunshot silenced him forever.

"Daboo? Yo, Daboo? Daboo," Jynx called after his comrade, but didn't get a response. He looked back at Parelli, who motioned him down the staircase with his pistol. Jynx, who was scared, swallowed his spit and made his way into the basement. Parelli cautiously followed behind him, with his gun at the ready.

The exchange of gunfire rang out from the basement and into the streets.

***

The overwhelming stench of piss, shit and blood lingered in the air, but it did little to hinder Rich Loc's very important mission. He was laser-focused on one thing, and one thing only, finding out who'd stolen his drugs and making their suffering legendary.

Rich Loc, wearing a blue bandana around the lower half of his face, circled his victims with a bloody chainsaw, covered in chunks of flesh and strands of hair. His forehead and muscular upper body shone from sweat and blood splatter. A half a dozen of his hitters, all armed with assault rifles, stood in the background, having watched the horrific scene unfold before their eyes only minutes prior. There was a total of four women hanging handcuffed from a pipe in the ceiling. Three of them were sweaty, sobbing and begging for their lives. The fourth, and final one, was dead and dripping blood onto the black garbage bags covering the basement's floor. Rich Loc had buried the chainsaw's blade into the side of her face, when she acted like she didn't know who'd stolen his product.

"Sooooo, I'm supposed to believe nobody knows anythang about what happened to my shit, cuz? Not nan' one of you hoes?" Rich Loc posed the question, as he circled his terrified victims for the second time. His chainsaw dripped blood on his sneakers and over the black garbage bags. One of the women was so scared she threw up a greenish-pink goo. Another one farted and shitted her panties. The last one fought back tears as she pleaded for him to spare their lives.

"Oh, please, please, Rich Loc, don't kill us. I'm beggin' you," she cried. She had a drenched face and snot sliding over her top lip. Her tears had ruined her eyeliner and makeup.

"You don't wanna die, then I suggest you bitchez start singin'," Rich Loc told them over the antagonizing noise of his chainsaw's blade.

The women quieted down, but there were still whimpers among them. They swallowed their spit and began to croon. This pissed Rich Loc off further. Scowling behind his bandana, he grunted and slammed the butt of his chainsaw into one of the women's forehead, splitting her shit to the white meat. Shorty's eyes cocked and blood spilled out of her wound. "Cuz, that's not what the fuck I meant. I mean snitch. Tell me who stole my product."

"But, Rich, we don't know who—who stole your—" The woman was interrupted by the infuriated buzzing of Rich Loc's chainsaw. The ladies screamed to the top of their lungs as he went down the row of them, cutting them in halves.

If it wasn't for the soundproof basement, the neighbors would have definitely heard the terrified screams of the kingpin's victims. Rich Loc narrowed his eyes into slits as blood sprayed his face and everywhere else. He didn't give a flying fuck that his victims were women. The way he saw it, they shouldn't have participated in stealing from him.

Once Rich Loc had finished with the deed, he tossed the chainsaw aside and pulled his bandana down from over his mouth. Wiping the mixture of blood and sweat from his forehead, he took the time to observe the mess he'd created, before heading for the staircase. He snatched the blue bandana from the waistband of one of his hitters and wiped the blood and sweat from his chest.

"Y'all clean up this mess and spread what's left of these bitchez throughout the city," Rich Loc told them, as he stood at the bottom of the staircase. He had one hand on the handrail and one foot on the bottom step. "I want my kingdom to know that if they should ever steal from their king, it's gon' be hell to pay. Ya dig?"

The hitters nodded and went to handle the task given to them. Rich Loc took the time to cup his hand around his mouth, as he sparked up a blunt. He blew out a cloud as he pocketed his blue Bic lighter. He'd gotten halfway up the staircase, when his cellphone started ringing. Switching hands with the blunt, he stopped at the basement door and answered the call. It was Gabby with some good news.

"A'ight, I love you more, queen." Rich Loc smiled wickedly and disconnected the call. He came up through the basement's door, thinking of ways he was going to torture the dumb son of a bitch that stole from him.

Chapter 19

The painful grunts of a man, sitting duct taped to a chair, bounced off the walls, whilst being savagely beaten. The hitters stood around, unmoved by the ass whooping the man had undoubtedly earned. In their line of business, they'd seen much worse happen to those who dared to cross Rich Loc. All of the hitters accounted for were holding assault rifles, but only a few of them were holding the chain leashes of Rottweilers.

Parelli, whose fists were wrapped in shiny metal chains, gave Cowboy a vicious three punch combination and stepped back. He stared him down, while sweat and blood slid down his hairy chest. Blood dripped from the chains wrapped around his fists and splashed on the floor.

Cowboy, who was bound to a chair at the center of a shower room of an old condemned high school, spat blood and looked up at Parelli defiantly. He had two blood clots in his left eye, his cheeks were swollen, his lips were busted and his face was covered in small, bloody cuts. Parelli had taken up the better part of an hour, trying to beat the whereabouts of the rest of Rich Loc's drugs out of him. But Cowboy proved to be as stubborn as a bull. He kept his mouth shut and took his punishment, like the soldier he was.

Back at Mariana's crib, shit got funky in the basement. The boy Jynx wound up taking two to the body. His body armor was able to stop a slug from piercing his chest, but the second one managed to hit him below the plate of his bulletproof vest. Cowboy swooped in to claim his life, but the Lord works in mysterious ways.

***

"Aaaaaah, ssssss!" Jynx hissed like a King Cobra, lying on his back and feeling for the wound below his body armor. When he touched it, his fingers came away bloody. He forgot all about his injury, when he saw the shadows stirring before him. The next thing he knew, Cowboy crept forward with both of his six shooters aimed at his forehead. He could tell by the look in his eyes, he was as high as Jupiter, but if anything, that only made him more dangerous.

"That was a sweet, innocent lady you killed," Cowboy said with his eyebrows slanted and nose wrinkled. "She wasn't in this game you and I play. She was a civilian. She was off limits. Should you see her on the other side, be sure to tell her I apologize for bringing my shit to her doorst—"

"If you don't drop those sticks, you'll be able to tell that old broad yo'self, face to face," Parelli interrupted, with his silenced barrel pressed against Cowboy's temple. Cowboy's eyes darted to their corners, taking in the masked man's appearance. "You seem to think I give a fuck about dying, my nigga. Me and ya man's can both go out this bitch in style, nah mean? When I'm gone, the streets gon' celebrate me as a legend."

There were the whispers of a deadly weapon and then came the stinging sensation in Cowboy's chest. He dropped his twin revolvers as he collided with the floor. He moved to recover one of them and it was shot out of his reach. Before he knew it, Jynx and Parelli were walking up on him with their infrared dots pinned on his forehead.

"Don't be stupid," Jynx told Cowboy between winces. He saw him glance at his other piece. He knew he was thinking about going for it, even under the threat of his opps' guns.

Sighing, Cowboy lay his head back against the floor and stared up at the ceiling. He didn't know what these fools wanted. He'd done mad shit to niggas in the streets, so this could be pay back for a number of things.

"I've never taken you for a dumb nigga," Parelli said, tucking his gun at the small of his back. He then pulled out a zip tie and a black hood.

***

Cowboy had the mother of all migraines and only an Aspirin the size of a hockey puck could get rid of it. On top of that, he was completely naked and aching all over. In addition to Parelli putting the beats on him, the hitters had sicced their Rottweilers on him. The beasts bit, gnawed and chewed on nearly every exposed area of his body and by the looks in their eyes, he could tell they wanted another helping of him.

"You got somethin' you wanna tell me now, big man?" Parelli asked, as he unwrapped the bloody chains from around his fists.

"Y—yeah," Cowboy told him, looking defeated and broken.

Parelli removed the last chain and let it drop to the floor. He turned around to Cowboy, smiling wickedly, loving the fact that he'd finally managed to break his will. "I'm all ears."

"Ya mom's got some bomb ass pussy, son." Cowboy threw his head back, laughing maniacally and stomping the only sneaker he had on.

Some of the hitters held back laughter for fear of retaliation. The wicked smile dissolved from Parelli's lips and was replaced with a mask of hatred. The look on his face made Cowboy laugh harder and louder, stomping his foot with exaggeration. He knew he'd gotten under Parelli's skin, and he wanted to rub it in his face.

"Shit's funny, huh? You think it's funny?" Parelli spat angrily, taking his gun from the front of his jeans and chambering a round into it. He pointed his stick at Cowboy's forehead, and was surprised when Rich Loc stepped into his path.

"Fall back, cuz, unless you know where this piece of shit is keepin' my product," Rich Loc told him. Parelli shook his head, no. "Then lower your blicky, nigga. 'Cause cuz not finna meet the big homie in the sky as long as he's harborin' that secret."

Parelli took a deep breath and tucked his gun in his waistband.

"Where's Jynx?" He looked at all the faces of the hitters but didn't see Jynx among them.

"He took one in the gut, while we were tryna capture this bitch-ass nigga behind you." Parelli nodded to Cowboy, whose head was lowered, staring him down. He looked like an evil spirit had taken possession of his body. "I dropped 'em off at home and made arrangements for Fitz to tend to 'em."

Rich Loc nodded as he slipped on a pair of black leather gloves and pulled them over his hands. He produced a taser from his pocket, as he walked towards Cowboy. He squeezed the sides of the black device and it crackled with electricity.

"Let's try this again," Rich Loc said to no one in particular, determined to make Cowboy talk.

***

Golden talked to the fire chief as his men fought the inferno consuming him and Aries' house. He stashed his piece underneath the house next door, since it was for sale and there wasn't anyone living in the place. Then he washed his hands in urine to get rid of the gunpowder residue. He was willing to bet two-inches of dick Jake was going to come around asking questions with all the gunfire earlier, and he was right as rain. The police popped out, pressing him and asking a million questions, to which he played dumb.

"Nah, I'm good, me and my girl will probably stay at a hotel or something," Golden told the fire chief. He gave him a nod and walked away to address his men.

Golden pulled out his cellphone to tell Aries what went down. As he scrolled through his contacts, his jack rang and vibrated in his hand. It was her.

"Babe, you not finna believe this shit—" Golden began, but he was quickly cut off.

"Bae, they caught up with yo' brother and I think they're about to kill 'em," Aries spat in a panic.

"Which brother? And who caught up with 'em?"

"Cowboy. And Rich. I told you he put up the dough for his whereabouts. Well, someone dropped by the bar today and gave up some info," Aries told him. "She gave up a name and a description."

"Fuck," Golden shouted furiously, drawing the attention of some of the bystanders and firefighters. He walked from out of their earshot and continued his conversation. "Who's the bitch that dropped dime?"

"Some ho named Jade."

"Junkie bitch." Golden closed his eyes briefly and shook his head.

Aries informed Golden she had put a GPS location app on Rich Loc's cellphone, so she knew where he was at all times. They made plans to link up, rally the Loves and execute a strike to get Cowboy back.

"G, what was it that you hadda tell me that I wouldn't believe?"

Golden, still holding his cellular to his ear, looked over his shoulder at what was left of their home. "I'll tell you later, shorty. Right now, we needa get going, so we can catch up with ya boy Rich."

"Okay. I love you."

"Dido."

Golden disconnected the call, hopped into his whip and backed out of the driveway.

***

Shirvetta, Biggie and Baby Girl were sitting in the living room, watching *Power,* when someone knocked at the door. They were so engrossed in the cable television show that no one wanted to answer the door.

"Get that, sis." Biggie nudged Baby Girl.

"Nah. It's your turn. I got it when the pizza came," Baby Girl replied, opening up the Dominoes box and taking another slice.

Biggie looked at Shirvetta, who was snuggled under a blanket on the opposite couch. "Boy, please, you're the man of the house, since your father isn't here, so you needa answer it."

Biggie took a breath, grabbed his gun off the coffee table and walked to the front door. He stole a peek through the peep-hole and saw his second oldest sibling standing on the other side.

"Who is it, Biggie?" Shirvetta asked.

"Golden," Biggie replied, unlocking the door and pulling it open. Golden stepped inside the house, pulling off his hood and looking over the living room. Biggie closed and locked the door behind him. He looked Golden over with a frown, taking in his all black attire.

"'Sup witchu, bro? You dressed up like you're about to put in some work," Biggie said.

"That's what I was about to say?" Baby Girl chimed in. She tossed what was left of her pizza into the box and smacked the crumbs off her hands.

"You look like somethin' is botherin' you. What's the matter, son?" Shirvetta asked with concern, throwing the blanket aside and rising from the sofa. She could tell by the scowl on Golden's face something was troubling him.

"Niggaz set me and Aries's crib on fire and shot it up," Golden replied.

"Oh my God, are you okay, baby?" Shirvetta approached, checking him for wounds. Baby Girl came from the opposite side of him, examining him for wounds also.

"I'm good, ma. Really," Golden assured Shirvetta, kissing her forehead. He turned to Baby Girl and kissed her on the cheek.

"Bro, you know how we roll. All you gotta do is point 'em out, and I'll make 'em a memory," Biggie told him. He didn't have a problem taking someone's life, and this situation gave him the perfect excuse.

"Honestly, I don't know," Golden admitted. "But listen, I'm not here for that. I'm here on the account of Cowboy. Rich Loc had some fools kidnap 'em and I think he plans on killin' 'em. We've gotta bust a move tonight."

Biggie scowled and waved him off. "Man, forget that nigga. He's on his own."

"What chu mean he's on his own? That's our big brother. He's blood," Golden countered.

"That nigga ceased being my brother after he put hands on Baby Girl, beat cho ass, and then threw ma across the room, like a rag doll," Biggie shot back. "If whoever has 'em decides to kill 'em, they'll be doin' me a favor, 'cause I fa sho' planned on doin' it myself."

"I can't believe this," Golden replied heatedly. "They got bruh over some mess we all participated in and you wanna leave 'em to be crucified? Son, I don't care what we go through internally, we're family. We can settle our differences later. But when outsiders start messin' with our own, they get dealt with, A-sap. Ya dig, baby brother?"

"Yeah. I dig. I'm still not budgin' though. I'm standin' on what I said, 'fuck Cowboy'," Biggie said.

Chapter 20

This was the first time Biggie had cussed in front of their mother, so Golden knew he was dead ass. There wasn't any way he could get him to change his mind, so he thought he'd try to persuade the women.

"Baby Girl, I know you got cho big brother back," Golden said, locking eyes with his sister.

Baby Girl went to step forward, but Biggie stepped in front of her, blocking her path. He shook his head, no. Baby Girl looked at Golden from over Biggie's shoulder with sorrowful eyes. She wasn't sure of what she should do. She wanted to roll out with Golden and get Cowboy back, but then again, she also wanted to stay on her twin's good side. They had a unique bond, seeing as how they were fraternal and came out of the same womb on the same day. Baby Girl dropped her head and fidgeted with her fingers.

"Ma, you gon' leave yo' son hangin'? Regardless of what Cowboy did, he's still one of your boys," Golden told Shirvetta, taking note of the hand impression on her neck from Cowboy choking her.

"Drop it, Golden. The nigga said it himself that mom's is not his real old lady. So, what does she look like ridin' out witchu to put the smash on whomever has that nigga?" Biggie interjected, pulling his mother behind him. She looked like she wanted to go with Golden, but there was something within her mind holding her back.

"My nigga, last time I checked, Shirvetta Love was a grown ass woman, who can speak for herself. Ma," Golden looked at his mother, hoping she'd come along on his rescue mission.

"Tell 'em you not goin' nowhere, ma. Tell 'em you refuse to bust yo' gun behind yo' illegitimate ass son, who put his hands on you. And don't chu feel bad about it either, 'cause that demon doesn't deserve a mother's love. As a matter of fact, son doesn't deserve anyone's love." Biggie's face was scrunched and a vein on his forehead was pronounced.

"Golden, I—" Shirvetta began, but she was cut off by Golden throwing up his hand.

"Spare me the excuses, ma, I don't need 'em," Golden said with teary eyes. "Y'all don't want to come with me to get Cowboy back? Cool. I'll do it my damn self, but if I get murdered in the process, just know it will be all y'all's fault." He motioned a finger around to all of them. "If you can live with that, then you never cared about me in the first place." Golden turned around, wiping the tears from his eyes, as he walked towards the front door.

"Bruh, you can't put that on us. Come on now. That ain't right, yo." Biggie said, starting to feel guilty.

Golden walked out of the house, leaving the front door wide open. He hopped over the gated fence with one hand and sped walked toward his whip.

"I'm not letting my baby go off alone. If something happens to 'em, I'll be sick," Shirvetta told Biggie, holding his chubby face in her hands. "Baby Girl, catch up with Golden and tell 'em we're comin' along. I'll be getting the armor and guns." She darted to the back of the house, where the armory was located.

Baby Girl went to chase after Golden, but Biggie grabbed her arm. She looked back at him like he'd called her out of her name.

"Stay outta that shit. Remember that nigga put his hands on you," Biggie said with a mad dog expression.

Baby Girl snatched her arm back and looked at him, angrily. "People make mistakes, Biggie. No one is perfect. Like Golden said, Cowboy's our brother. If someone's gonna hurt 'em, then they're gonna have to see all of us behind that."

Baby Girl ran out of the house as fast as she could, calling after Golden, hoping to catch up with him.

"Golden, wait, wait. We're coming with you."

Urrrrk!

Golden busted a U-turn in the middle of the street, speeding past Baby Girl, without looking her way.

A second later, Shirvetta ran out of the house wearing a bulletproof-vest over her wife beater. She ran out into the middle of the residential street, looking down the block at the back lights of Golden's vehicle.

"Golden. Gollllldennn," Shirvetta called after him until the rear lights of his car disappeared. Baby Girl ran out of the yard and stood beside her. Shirvetta wrapped her arms around her and they continued to stare down the block, where Golden's whip vanished

"Ma, I hope he'll be okay," Baby Girl said with glassy-eyes.

"Me too, baby. Me too," Shirvetta replied, taking an exasperated breath.

Biggie stood in the doorway, watching the entire scene unfold. He lingered there a moment longer, before walking back in the house.

***

Aries stared out of the passenger window as she waited for Golden. Her heart was beating fast and her palms were clammy. She was nervous about the possibilities that night. Golden was expecting her to kick down the door of wherever Cowboy was being held with guns blazing. But she was terrified Rich Loc would wind up getting killed in the process. She loved Rich Loc, just as much as she loved Golden, and she'd die knowing she was involved with his being murdered. She didn't know how she was going to do it, but she had to lure Rich Loc from the spot before her and the Loves hit the place.

Come on, bitch! Think, think, think, Aries thought. She looked at the driver's door when she saw Golden's reflection in the passenger window. He slid in behind the wheel and slammed the door shut. Aries's forehead wrinkled seeing him frowning and glassy-eyed. She'd expected him to return with his family for their mission but he'd come back alone. She knew then that something had gone down.

"G, what happened in there?" Aries asked.

"What happened is, my muthafuckin' family is leaving my brother for dead. I can't believe this shit." Golden slammed his fist on the dashboard in a fit of anger. He cranked up his whip, pulled away from the curb and busted a U-turn in the middle of the street. Aries looked through the driver's window, to see Baby Girl running out of the house, calling his name.

"Babe, your sister's calling after you. Maybe they changed their minds about coming along," Aries told him.

Golden kept his attention focused on the road ahead. "Fuck them. It's too late now. It's just you and me, ma. You got my back, right?" Golden glanced at her.

"You know I got chu, 'til the very end," Aries assured him, interlocking her fingers with his and kissing his hand. He grinned and kissed her hand back.

A'ight, big bruh, hang tight, the cavalry is on the way, Golden thought, zipping up the street and leaving debris in his wake.

***

Heavy's eyes popped open as he gasped for air. His face was covered in sweat bubbles and fear was prevalent in his eyes. He took his contraband cellphone from its hiding place and slid off his bunk. His new cellie sat up on his bunk, frowning and rubbing his eye. He'd heard Heavy making noise in his sleep and figured he'd had a nightmare. They'd gotten rather close during his short time there, so he was concerned with his well-being.

"Yo, main man, what's the deal?" Quentin asked groggily.

"Calling home, bruh. I just hadda nightmare I hope doesn't come true," Heavy replied, holding his cellular to his ear and pacing the floor. "Come on, Goddess, pick up," he said under his breath, referring to Shirvetta.

"I'm not tryna be all up in yours, main man, but what was ya nightmare about?" Quentin yawned, stretching his arms and legs.

"One of my kids, man," Heavy replied, disconnecting the call and hitting Shirvetta again.

"What about one of your kids?"

"One of them was killed in my nightmare, and that shit felt so real."

***

Cowboy had urinated and defecated on himself, after Rich Loc tased him so many times. His heart was beating funny and he experienced occasional tremors. Still, he didn't fold under the intense scrutiny and unbearable pain.

"You're one bad muthafucka, son. You know that? My locs and I have never hadda work this hard to get a vic to crack. You should consider this an honor, me having to use my girls and all. Yep. It's been a long time since me and the ladies have been out on a date." Rich Loc sat a length of velvet the size of a small rug on an end table. He drew its string and rolled it open. He feasted his eyes on a set of unique knives with diamond dust edges and spiked knuckle guards. Each blade had its own name engraved on it in

Arabic. A devilish smile graced Rich Loc's lips, when he saw his reflection in the weapons of torture.

Cowboy watched as Rich Loc removed all of his jewelry and set it aside on the end table. He pulled his shirt over his head and tossed it aside. He removed a blue bandana from his left back pocket and tied it around the lower half of his face. Next, he put on a pair of black latex gloves and picked up the biggest knife in his collection. Staring at his reflection in the blade, Rich Loc fixed his hair and checked his teeth for any food that may be stuck between them.

"You come anywhere near me with that knife, and I'ma bend you over and fuck you with it," Cowboy swore.

"My dogs are hungry, real hungry, so each time you refuse to tell me what I wanna know, I'm gonna slice off a part of you and feed it to 'em," Rich Loc told him. "I think I'll start with your left ear. Yeah. The left ear will be juuuust perfect," he licked his top row of teeth as he walked towards Cowboy, to make good on his threat. The hounds his hitters held on leashes licked their chops in anticipation of being fed parts of Cowboy.

Cowboy grunted as he rocked back and forth in the chair, trying desperately to get free.

To Be Continued

MY SELF-PUBLISHED BOOKS

BLOODY KNUCKLES
THE DEVIL WEARS TIMBS 1-7
ME AND MY HITTAZ 1-6
THE LAST REAL NIGGA ALIVE 1-3
A HOOD NIGGA'S BLUES
A SOUTH CENTRAL LOVE AFFAIR

Lock Down Publications and Ca$h Presents Assisted Publishing Packages

BASIC PACKAGE $499 Editing Cover Design Formatting	UPGRADED PACKAGE $800 Typing Editing Cover Design Formatting
ADVANCE PACKAGE $1,200 Typing Editing Cover Design Formatting Copyright registration Proofreading Upload book to Amazon	LDP SUPREME PACKAGE $1,500 Typing Editing Cover Design Formatting Copyright registration Proofreading Set up Amazon account Upload book to Amazon Advertise on LDP, Amazon and Facebook Page

***Other services available upon request.
Additional charges may apply

Lock Down Publications
P.O. Box 944
Stockbridge, GA 30281-9998
Phone: 470 303-9761

Submission Guideline

Submit the first three chapters of your completed manuscript to ldpsubmissions@gmail.com. In the subject line add **Your Book's Title**. The manuscript must be in a Word Doc file and sent as an attachment. Document should be in Times New Roman, double spaced, and in size 12 font. Also, provide your synopsis and full contact information. If sending multiple submissions, they must each be in a separate email.

Have a story but no way to send it electronically? You can still submit to LDP/Ca$h Presents. Send in the first three chapters, written or typed, of your completed manuscript to:

LDP: Submissions Dept
P.O. Box 944
Stockbridge, GA 30281-9998

DO NOT send original manuscript. Must be a duplicate. Provide your synopsis and a cover letter containing your full contact information.

Thanks for considering LDP and Ca$h Presents.

NEW RELEASES

BLOODLINE OF A SAVAGE **BY PRINCE A. TAUHID**

THE MURDER QUEENS 4 **BY MICHAEL GALLON**

THE BUTTERFLY MAFIA **BY FUMIYA PAYNE**

KING KILLA 2 **BY VINCENT "VITTO" HOLLOWAY**

BABY, I'M WINTERTIME COLD 3 **BY MEESHA**

THESE VICIOUS STREETS **BY PRINCE A. TAUHID**

TIL DEATH 2 **BY ARYANNA**

CITY OF SMOKE 2 **BY MOLOTTI**

STEPPERS **BY KING RIO**

THE LANE **BY KEN-KEN SPENCE**

MONEY GAME 2 **BY SMOOVE DOLLA**

THE BLACK DIAMOND CARTEL **BY SAYNOMORE**

CRIME BOSS 2 **BY PLAYA RAY**

THUG OF SPADES **BY COREY ROBINSON**

LOVE IN THE TRENCHES 2 **BY COREY ROBINSON**

TIL DEATH 3 **BY ARYANNA**

THE BIRTH OF A GANGSTER 4 **BY DELMONT PLAYER**

PRODUCT OF THE STREETS **BY DEMOND "MONEY" ANDERSON**

Coming Soon from Lock Down Publications/Ca$h Presents

BLOOD OF A BOSS VI
SHADOWS OF THE GAME II
TRAP BASTARD II
By **Askari**

LOYAL TO THE GAME IV
By **T.J. & Jelissa**

TRUE SAVAGE VIII
MIDNIGHT CARTEL IV
DOPE BOY MAGIC IV
CITY OF KINGZ III
NIGHTMARE ON SILENT AVE II
THE PLUG OF LIL MEXICO II
CLASSIC CITY II
By **Chris Green**

BLAST FOR ME III
A SAVAGE DOPEBOY III
CUTTHROAT MAFIA III
DUFFLE BAG CARTEL VII
HEARTLESS GOON VI
By **Ghost**

A HUSTLER'S DECEIT III
KILL ZONE II
BAE BELONGS TO ME III
TIL DEATH II
By **Aryanna**

KING OF THE TRAP III
By **T.J. Edwards**

GORILLAZ IN THE BAY V
3X KRAZY III
STRAIGHT BEAST MODE III
By **De'Kari**

KINGPIN KILLAZ IV
STREET KINGS III
PAID IN BLOOD III
CARTEL KILLAZ IV
DOPE GODS III
By **Hood Rich**

SINS OF A HUSTLA II
By **ASAD**

YAYO V
BRED IN THE GAME 2
By **S. Allen**

THE STREETS WILL TALK II
By **Yolanda Moore**

SON OF A DOPE FIEND III
HEAVEN GOT A GHETTO III
SKI MASK MONEY III
By **Renta**

LOYALTY AIN'T PROMISED III
By **Keith Williams**

I'M NOTHING WITHOUT HIS LOVE II
SINS OF A THUG II
TO THE THUG I LOVED BEFORE II
IN A HUSTLER I TRUST II
By **Monet Dragun**

QUIET MONEY IV
EXTENDED CLIP III
THUG LIFE IV
By **Trai'Quan**

THE STREETS MADE ME IV
By **Larry D. Wright**

IF YOU CROSS ME ONCE III
ANGEL V
By **Anthony Fields**

THE STREETS WILL NEVER CLOSE IV
By **K'ajji**

HARD AND RUTHLESS III
KILLA KOUNTY IV
By **Khufu**

MONEY GAME III
By **Smoove Dolla**

MURDA WAS THE CASE III
Elijah R. Freeman

AN UNFORESEEN LOVE IV
BABY, I'M WINTERTIME COLD III
By **Meesha**

QUEEN OF THE ZOO III
By **Black Migo**

CONFESSIONS OF A JACKBOY III
By **Nicholas Lock**

JACK BOYS VS DOPE BOYS IV
A GANGSTA'S QUR'AN V
COKE GIRLZ II
COKE BOYS II
LIFE OF A SAVAGE V
CHI'RAQ GANGSTAS V
SOSA GANG III
BRONX SAVAGES II
BODYMORE KINGPINS II
By **Romell Tukes**

KING KILLA II
By **Vincent "Vitto" Holloway**

BETRAYAL OF A THUG III
By **Fre$h**

THE MURDER QUEENS III
By **Michael Gallon**

THE BIRTH OF A GANGSTER III
By **Delmont Player**

TREAL LOVE II
By **Le'Monica Jackson**

FOR THE LOVE OF BLOOD III
By **Jamel Mitchell**

RAN OFF ON DA PLUG II
By **Paper Boi Rari**

HOOD CONSIGLIERE III
By **Keese**

PRETTY GIRLS DO NASTY THINGS II
By **Nicole Goosby**

PROTÉGÉ OF A LEGEND III
LOVE IN THE TRENCHES II
By **Corey Robinson**

IT'S JUST ME AND YOU II
By **Ah'Million**

FOREVER GANGSTA III
By **Adrian Dulan**

GORILLAZ IN THE TRENCHES II
By **SayNoMore**

THE COCAINE PRINCESS VIII
By **King Rio**

CRIME BOSS II
By **Playa Ray**

LOYALTY IS EVERYTHING III
By **Molotti**

HERE TODAY GONE TOMORROW II
By **Fly Rock**

REAL G'S MOVE IN SILENCE II
By **Von Diesel**

GRIMEY WAYS IV
By **Ray Vinci**

Available Now

RESTRAINING ORDER I & II
By **CA$H & Coffee**

LOVE KNOWS NO BOUNDARIES I II & III
By **Coffee**

RAISED AS A GOON I, II, III & IV
BRED BY THE SLUMS I, II, III
BLAST FOR ME I & II
ROTTEN TO THE CORE I II III
A BRONX TALE I, II, III
DUFFLE BAG CARTEL I II III IV V VI
HEARTLESS GOON I II III IV V
A SAVAGE DOPEBOY I II
DRUG LORDS I II III
CUTTHROAT MAFIA I II
KING OF THE TRENCHES
By **Ghost**

LAY IT DOWN I & II
LAST OF A DYING BREED I II
BLOOD STAINS OF A SHOTTA I & II III
By **Jamaica**

LOYAL TO THE GAME I II III
LIFE OF SIN I, II III
By **TJ & Jelissa**

IF LOVING HIM IS WRONG…I & II
LOVE ME EVEN WHEN IT HURTS I II III
By **Jelissa**

BLOODY COMMAS I & II
SKI MASK CARTEL I, II & III
KING OF NEW YORK I II, III IV V
RISE TO POWER I II III
COKE KINGS I II III IV V
BORN HEARTLESS I II III IV
KING OF THE TRAP I II
By **T.J. Edwards**

WHEN THE STREETS CLAP BACK I & II III
THE HEART OF A SAVAGE I II III IV
MONEY MAFIA I II
LOYAL TO THE SOIL I II III
By **Jibril Williams**

A DISTINGUISHED THUG STOLE MY HEART I II & III
LOVE SHOULDN'T HURT I II III IV
RENEGADE BOYS I II III IV
PAID IN KARMA I II III
SAVAGE STORMS I II III
AN UNFORESEEN LOVE I II III
BABY, I'M WINTERTIME COLD I II
By **Meesha**

A GANGSTER'S CODE I &, II III
A GANGSTER'S SYN I II III
THE SAVAGE LIFE I II III
CHAINED TO THE STREETS I II III
BLOOD ON THE MONEY I II III
A GANGSTA'S PAIN I II III
By **J-Blunt**

PUSH IT TO THE LIMIT
By **Bre' Hayes**

BLOOD OF A BOSS I, II, III, IV, V
SHADOWS OF THE GAME
TRAP BASTARD
By **Askari**

THE STREETS BLEED MURDER I, II & III
THE HEART OF A GANGSTA I II& III
By **Jerry Jackson**

CUM FOR ME I II III IV V VI VII VIII
An **LDP Erotica Collaboration**

BRIDE OF A HUSTLA I II & II
THE FETTI GIRLS I, II& III
CORRUPTED BY A GANGSTA I, II III, IV
BLINDED BY HIS LOVE
THE PRICE YOU PAY FOR LOVE I, II ,III
DOPE GIRL MAGIC I II III
By **Destiny Skai**

WHEN A GOOD GIRL GOES BAD
By **Adrienne**

A GANGSTER'S REVENGE I II III & IV
THE BOSS MAN'S DAUGHTERS I II III IV V
A SAVAGE LOVE I & II
BAE BELONGS TO ME I II
A HUSTLER'S DECEIT I, II, III
WHAT BAD BITCHES DO I, II, III
SOUL OF A MONSTER I II III
KILL ZONE
A DOPE BOY'S QUEEN I II III
TIL DEATH
By **Aryanna**

THE COST OF LOYALTY I II III
By **Kweli**

A KINGPIN'S AMBITION
A KINGPIN'S AMBITION **II**
I MURDER FOR THE DOUGH
By **Ambitious**

TRUE SAVAGE I II III IV V VI VII
DOPE BOY MAGIC I, II, III
MIDNIGHT CARTEL I II III
CITY OF KINGZ I II
NIGHTMARE ON SILENT AVE
THE PLUG OF LIL MEXICO II
CLASSIC CITY
By **Chris Green**

A DOPEBOY'S PRAYER
By **Eddie "Wolf" Lee**

THE KING CARTEL I, II & III
By **Frank Gresham**

THESE NIGGAS AIN'T LOYAL I, II & III
By **Nikki Tee**

GANGSTA SHYT I II &III
By **CATO**

THE ULTIMATE BETRAYAL
By **Phoenix**

BOSS'N UP I, II & III
By **Royal Nicole**

I LOVE YOU TO DEATH
By **Destiny J**

I RIDE FOR MY HITTA
I STILL RIDE FOR MY HITTA
By **Misty Holt**

LOVE & CHASIN' PAPER
By **Qay Crockett**

TO DIE IN VAIN
SINS OF A HUSTLA
By **ASAD**

BROOKLYN HUSTLAZ
By **Boogsy Morina**

BROOKLYN ON LOCK I & II
By **Sonovia**

GANGSTA CITY
By **Teddy Duke**

A DRUG KING AND HIS DIAMOND I & II III
A DOPEMAN'S RICHES
HER MAN, MINE'S TOO I, II
CASH MONEY HO'S
THE WIFEY I USED TO BE I II
PRETTY GIRLS DO NASTY THINGS
By Nicole Goosby

LIPSTICK KILLAH I, II, III
CRIME OF PASSION I II & III
FRIEND OR FOE I II III
By **Mimi**

TRAPHOUSE KING I II & III
KINGPIN KILLAZ I II III
STREET KINGS I II
PAID IN BLOOD I II
CARTEL KILLAZ I II III
DOPE GODS I II
By **Hood Rich**

STEADY MOBBN' I, II, III
THE STREETS STAINED MY SOUL I II III
By **Marcellus Allen**

WHO SHOT YA I, II, III
SON OF A DOPE FIEND I II
HEAVEN GOT A GHETTO I II
SKI MASK MONEY I II
By **Renta**

GORILLAZ IN THE BAY I II III IV
TEARS OF A GANGSTA I II
3X KRAZY I II
STRAIGHT BEAST MODE I II
By **DE'KARI**

TRIGGADALE I II III
MURDA WAS THE CASE I II
By **Elijah R. Freeman**

THE STREETS ARE CALLING
By **Duquie Wilson**

SLAUGHTER GANG I II III
RUTHLESS HEART I II III
By **Willie Slaughter**

MONEY HUNGRY DEMONS | TRANAY ADAMS

GOD BLESS THE TRAPPERS I, II, III
THESE SCANDALOUS STREETS I, II, III
FEAR MY GANGSTA I, II, III IV, V
THESE STREETS DON'T LOVE NOBODY I, II
BURY ME A G I, II, III, IV, V
A GANGSTA'S EMPIRE I, II, III, IV
THE DOPEMAN'S BODYGAURD I II
THE REALEST KILLAZ I II III
THE LAST OF THE OGS I II III
By **Tranay Adams**

MARRIED TO A BOSS I II III
By **Destiny Skai & Chris Green**

KINGZ OF THE GAME I II III IV V VI VII
CRIME BOSS
By **Playa Ray**

FUK SHYT
By **Blakk Diamond**

DON'T F#CK WITH MY HEART I II
By **Linnea**

ADDICTED TO THE DRAMA I II III
IN THE ARM OF HIS BOSS II
By **Jamila**

YAYO I II III IV
A SHOOTER'S AMBITION I II
BRED IN THE GAME
By **S. Allen**

LOYALTY AIN'T PROMISED I II
By **Keith Williams**

TRAP GOD I II III
RICH $AVAGE I II III
MONEY IN THE GRAVE I II III
By **Martell Troublesome Bolden**

FOREVER GANGSTA I II
GLOCKS ON SATIN SHEETS I II
By **Adrian Dulan**

TOE TAGZ I II III IV
LEVELS TO THIS SHYT I II
IT'S JUST ME AND YOU
By **Ah'Million**

KINGPIN DREAMS I II III
RAN OFF ON DA PLUG
By **Paper Boi Rari**

CONFESSIONS OF A GANGSTA I II III IV
CONFESSIONS OF A JACKBOY I II
By **Nicholas Lock**

I'M NOTHING WITHOUT HIS LOVE
SINS OF A THUG
TO THE THUG I LOVED BEFORE
A GANGSTA SAVED XMAS
IN A HUSTLER I TRUST
By **Monet Dragun**

QUIET MONEY I II III
THUG LIFE I II III
EXTENDED CLIP I II
A GANGSTA'S PARADISE
By **Trai'Quan**

CAUGHT UP IN THE LIFE I II III
THE STREETS NEVER LET GO I II III
By **Robert Baptiste**

NEW TO THE GAME I II III
MONEY, MURDER & MEMORIES I II III
By **Malik D. Rice**

CREAM I II III
THE STREETS WILL TALK
By **Yolanda Moore**

LIFE OF A SAVAGE I II III IV
A GANGSTA'S QUR'AN I II III IV
MURDA SEASON I II III
GANGLAND CARTEL I II III
CHI'RAQ GANGSTAS I II III IV
KILLERS ON ELM STREET I II III
JACK BOYZ N DA BRONX I II III
A DOPEBOY'S DREAM I II III
JACK BOYS VS DOPE BOYS I II III
COKE GIRLZ
COKE BOYS
SOSA GANG I II
BRONX SAVAGES
BODYMORE KINGPINS
By **Romell Tukes**

THE STREETS MADE ME I II III
By **Larry D. Wright**

CONCRETE KILLA I II III
VICIOUS LOYALTY I II III
By **Kingpen**

THE ULTIMATE SACRIFICE I, II, III, IV, V, VI
KHADIFI
IF YOU CROSS ME ONCE I II
ANGEL I II III IV
IN THE BLINK OF AN EYE
By **Anthony Fields**

THE LIFE OF A HOOD STAR
By **Ca$h & Rashia Wilson**

THE STREETS WILL NEVER CLOSE I II III
By **K'ajji**

NIGHTMARES OF A HUSTLA I II III
By **King Dream**

HARD AND RUTHLESS I II
MOB TOWN 251
THE BILLIONAIRE BENTLEYS I II III
REAL G'S MOVE IN SILENCE
By **Von Diesel**

GHOST MOB
By **Stilloan Robinson**

MOB TIES I II III IV V VI
SOUL OF A HUSTLER, HEART OF A KILLER I II
GORILLAZ IN THE TRENCHES
By **SayNoMore**

BODYMORE MURDERLAND I II III
THE BIRTH OF A GANGSTER I II
By **Delmont Player**

FOR THE LOVE OF A BOSS
By **C. D. Blue**

KILLA KOUNTY I II III IV
By Khufu

MOBBED UP I II III IV
THE BRICK MAN I II III IV V
THE COCAINE PRINCESS I II III IV V VI VII
By **King Rio**

MONEY GAME I II
By **Smoove Dolla**

A GANGSTA'S KARMA I II III
By **FLAME**

KING OF THE TRENCHES I II III
By **GHOST & TRANAY ADAMS**

QUEEN OF THE ZOO I II
By **Black Migo**

GRIMEY WAYS I II III
By **Ray Vinci**

XMAS WITH AN ATL SHOOTER
By **Ca$h & Destiny Skai**

KING KILLA
By **Vincent "Vitto" Holloway**

BETRAYAL OF A THUG I II
By **Fre$h**

MONEY HUNGRY DEMONS | TRANAY ADAMS

THE MURDER QUEENS I II
By **Michael Gallon**

TREAL LOVE
By **Le'Monica Jackson**

FOR THE LOVE OF BLOOD I II
By **Jamel Mitchell**

HOOD CONSIGLIERE I II
By **Keese**

PROTÉGÉ OF A LEGEND I II
LOVE IN THE TRENCHES
By **Corey Robinson**

BORN IN THE GRAVE I II III
By **Self Made Tay**

MOAN IN MY MOUTH
By **XTASY**

TORN BETWEEN A GANGSTER AND A GENTLEMAN
By **J-BLUNT & Miss Kim**

LOYALTY IS EVERYTHING I II
By **Molotti**

HERE TODAY GONE TOMORROW
By **Fly Rock**

PILLOW PRINCESS
By **S. Hawkins**

SANCTIFIED AND HORNY
by **XTASY**

THE PLUG OF LIL MEXICO 2
by **CHRIS GREEN**

THE BLACK DIAMOND CARTEL
by **SAYNOMORE**

THE BIRTH OF A GANGSTER 3
by **DELMONT PLAYER**

BOOKS BY LDP'S CEO, CA$H

TRUST IN NO MAN
TRUST IN NO MAN 2
TRUST IN NO MAN 3
BONDED BY BLOOD
SHORTY GOT A THUG
THUGS CRY
THUGS CRY 2
THUGS CRY 3
TRUST NO BITCH
TRUST NO BITCH 2
TRUST NO BITCH 3
TIL MY CASKET DROPS
RESTRAINING ORDER
RESTRAINING ORDER 2
IN LOVE WITH A CONVICT
LIFE OF A HOOD STAR
XMAS WITH AN ATL SHOOTER